Summer of Little Rain

Cut down the groves and the streams will vanish
—JOHN MUIR

SUMMER OF LITTLE RAIN

by Aileen Fisher

DRAWINGS BY GLORIA STEVENS

THOMAS NELSON & SONS
NEW YORK

Edinburgh   *Toronto*

Library of Congress Catalog Card Number: 61–6806

PRINTED IN THE UNITED STATES OF AMERICA

TO

Elizabeth Tompkins

Contents

Trouble in the Mountain Valley   9

The Freak Storm   33

Narrow Escape   52

The Shrinking Pond   72

A Break in the Drought   92

Dangerous Journey   113

Let Winter Come   135

Summer of Little Rain

Trouble in the Mountain Valley

1

SOMETHING HAD GONE WRONG in the mountain valley on the east side of the Rockies.

Of all the wild folk living in the high valley or ranging through it, the Beaver and her family were the first to be affected by the changes. For more than five months they had lived in safety and comfort in the dim world beneath the ice of the beaver pond. Now, with April half gone, they faced disturbing conditions they had never encountered before.

There were nine beavers: the mother and her mate, three two-year-olds, and four yearlings. From the time the pond froze over in early November, they had eaten and slept and groomed themselves in their low-domed house, and had sported and bathed in the pond, with hardly a care in the world.

Their food pile of aspen branches and sections of aspen trunks, carefully anchored in the mud at the bottom of the pond, lay handy to their house. The thick frozen walls of their mud-and-stick house had kept out enemies and winter storms. They had been safe. But now, with warm weather only a few weeks away, the ice was closing in on them like a trap!

Outwardly the valley looked as it always did in early spring. Slim gray aspens, climbing the slope south of the beaver pond, waded knee-deep in snow. Drifts still imprisoned the lower branches of spruces and firs in the dark woods that stretched northward beyond the marsh. The top of the beaver house humped out of an ice-locked pond.

Yet, for all the appearance of winter lingering on into April, the dry year had already begun. Here, almost ten thousand feet above sea level, where more snow usually fell than anywhere else in the mountains, the snowpack was only half its normal depth.

Months would pass before the beaver pond would feel the full effects of the smaller snowpack. But already other forces were at work changing the valley slowly but surely. In mid-April, the beavers, sealed in under the ice, were facing starvation.

During March the spring that welled up in the bottom of the beaver pond had begun to fail. Day by day feebler trickles of water bubbled up out of the mud between the storage pile and the tunnel to the lodge. As the flow diminished, the Beaver's mate dug around the spring, trying to bring it back to life. For a time he succeeded but lately, no matter how deep he dug, water refused to come.

Because of this underground water source, the Beaver's grandfather had built the lodge there in the first place. The warm water oozing out of the good earth kept thick ice from forming between the beaver house and the winter food pile, and so, in spite of what might happen in the white and frozen world outside, the colony could reach its supply of life-sustaining aspen bark.

Now, for the first time, the spring was dry. And without the flow of warm water, nothing could hold back the encroaching ice. All winter long, strong winds tearing down from the heights kept blowing away whatever snow fell on the pond. One below-zero spell after another had made the ice-roof thicker and thicker. Slowly, relentlessly, as the flow of the spring diminished, ice began forming around the food pile. Finally it was locked away in a solid block of ice—so near and yet so inaccessible.

Quite unknown to the beavers, the trouble had started two years before, at the head of the valley about a mile above their pond.

Some hikers, spending a week in the mountains before snow and cold closed the passes, had camped in early September at the foot of rugged peaks, where the forest of Engelmann spruces and alpine firs spread into a natural amphitheater. The campers were careful not to build a fire near fallen needles in the driest season of the mountain year. Choosing a small opening near the stream, they built their fire against a great gray boulder, on the open side.

For several hours that night they kept the fire blazing while they sat and talked. Then they doused it with water before crawling into their sleeping bags.

Eager to climb the rocky trail to the continental divide early the next morning, they took time to build only a small fire on the remains of the old one. This fire they put out, covering the ashes with stones before strapping on their packs and heading for the heights.

The campers did not realize that their evening fire had worked its way under old weeds and debris caught around the base of the boulder. All night a smouldering fire burned there without breaking into flames. The next day a breeze stirred it to life. Fingers of flame crept through the dry grass toward the needle-carpet under nearby trees.

Not until late afternoon did enough smoke billow up to show above the tops of the tall spruces. The watcher at the nearest fire lookout, eight miles to the south, gave the warning. About the same time the fire was spotted from the lookout fifteen miles to the north. But even with the fire pin-pointed, it posed a problem.

No roads led into the high valley, and it took several hours to assemble men and transport them and fire-fighting equipment to the nearest trail. Unfortunately the trails had not been cleared of fallen timber for a year or more. The going was slow for horses and men.

Meanwhile, fanned by increasing winds, flames leaped and roared through the timber. Fire and hot ashes ate into the mat of accumulated needles, cones, bark, and branches on the forest floor. Not until late the next morning were the first fire-fighters able to reach the head of the valley. Later a helicopter dropped more men and equipment by parachute.

The wind kept blowing, the fire kept spreading. Trees crashed, flames roared through pitchy branches, sparks scattered in showers. Ashes and smoke drifted as far east as the beaver pond, and farther. Terrified by the noise and smoke and leaping flames, wild folk fled down the valley.

Several days passed before the fire was under control. By then a great semicircular swath of forest had been ruined.

All this the beavers could not know. But the Beaver and her mate knew at the time, from the smell of smoke and the scum of ashes on the pond, that a fire raged somewhere nearby. And as the months passed they sensed that something drastic was happening to their valley. Why had their spring gone dry?

They had no way of knowing that when the big trees at the head of the valley went down in the fire, trouble started for their spring a mile away.

Every year the forest had caught quantities of snow in winter, holding drifts under its shadowy roof of branches until early summer. Matted needles and decomposing litter under the trees formed a thick brown carpet, a great blotter to soak up melting snow and rain. The blotter in turn fed underground water sources as the moisture slowly worked its way through fissures and cracks in the rocks. One of these fissures led to the beavers' spring.

With the protecting trees and forest carpet ruined by fire and the slope eroded during the next summer's rains, the sources of the underground spring soon began to suffer. Nothing was left at the head of the valley to hold moisture. By late winter of the second year after the fire, not enough water seeped down to feed the spring in the beaver pond.

What underground moisture still came had dropped in level, meeting a seam of water originating in the woods north of the pond. This seam ran more than a foot below the bottom of the pond, to the right of the old spring, and came to the surface below the beaver dam.

Had the beavers known about this seam of water, they could have dug it out and saved their pile of sunken aspen branches from the deepening ice.

The forest fire had another effect on the beaver pond that winter and spring before the drought. Always before, the great trees had served as a windbreak, slowing down the freezing winds that rushed from the heights.

With the trees gone, the pond felt the full force of the wind as it funneled down the mountain valley. Snow, that in other years covered the pond for a good part of the winter, went swirling away time after time. Without the warmth of its snow-blanket, the ice froze deeper than ever before.

On this morning in mid-April, the Beaver kept glancing toward the tunnel that led to the pond, as she rested in the lodge near her sleeping youngsters. They lay curled in their

beds, their scaly flat tails on edge against their sides. Where were they to get their next meal?

This was the time of year when the Beaver craved more food than usual—she was expecting a litter of kits by early June. Besides, she felt concern for the yearlings and two-year-olds growing thin before her eyes.

She was used to being imprisoned for six months of the year in a fortress of ice, away from the light, away from the sun. But never before in her seven years of life had she known the gnawing pain of hunger. Never before had so much of the pond frozen from top to bottom.

In the storage pile behind those glassy walls, aspen branches were still fresh, the bark juicy and full of life-giving nourishment. But how could the beavers reach them?

She sat up in the dark room, full of beaver smell, and mechanically began to groom herself. This was not easy in a mud-plastered room with a mud-and-clay floor. She yearned for the day when she could climb to the top of the beaver house and sun herself again. Better yet would be the day she could lie on an anthill and let the ants swarm over her and clean her fur of parasites. Best of all would be her first spring feast of tender shoots and grass!

Impatiently she sniffed at the stuffy air in the beaver house. She yearned almost as much for fresh air as for food. In the lodge, and under the ice of the pond, the cold staleness of winter air hung heavy. The thick walls of the lodge were frozen to such stony hardness no mountain lion or coyote could break through, but security came at a price. The tiny air vents at the top of the dome, where sticks were criss-crossed and plastered more loosely than in the walls, had become clogged with snow and ice. Scarcely a whiff of fresh-ness entered.

The air in the pond, in the space between water and ice, was no better. Without the freshening flow of the spring water, the pond lacked oxygen. Always before, the inflowing water had released enough oxygen to keep the air good for breathing.

Lack of food and lack of fresh air were a bad com-bination. The Beaver had noticed for several days that her young ones had become listless. Food must be found! Already the beavers had nibbled all the exposed willow twigs in the walls of their house and the lining of the tunnel. They dared not weaken the walls further. They had even eaten the old grass and shredded bark of their beds.

The Beaver stopped combing her fur and turned her eyes to the tunnel-door in the middle of the mud floor. She must go to the pond again and join her mate. He had been working alone for a long time.

Quietly she slid headfirst into the tunnel which led diagonally through the massive mud-and-stick foundation of the lodge to the bottom of the pond. The water in the tunnel was a shade lighter than the darkness of the room she had left. This meant that another day had broken over the valley and that light was filtering faintly through the thick ice.

In the dark hours of early morning the Beaver had helped her mate work on canals in the mud of the pond bottom, as they searched for rootstocks of water lilies and roots of other water plants. They had dug a small new canal to the bank at the deep end of the pond near their old summer burrow. Here they found a few tubers to bring back for the family to nibble.

Work on the canal was tiring; she not only had to dig, but to carry away the mud so the swimming space in the already cramped quarters of the pond would not become cluttered. After a time the Beaver had gone back to the lodge to rest. Now she was returning to dig again.

Enough light filtered through the ice to bring her some news of the outside world. She could see that the day was sunny. When sun glared down, the water under the ice-roof showed glints of darting light.

Her eyes were not made to see colors. Sunlight registered as shine and shimmer, not as yellow or gold. Shadows lay as patches of black or dark gray, without tints of purple and blue. Aspen bark was gray, without the delicate tinge of silver green that sets it apart from the bark of other light-colored trees.

But, as if to make up for her lack of color sense, the Beaver's ears and nose were unusually sensitive. By the sound of the water in the pond she could tell a great deal about what was happening. She knew at once that her mate was chipping away at the ice again, chipping at the wall around the storage pile.

She swam directly to him, leaving behind a trail of bubbles from the air held in her fur.

Her mate's long, chisel-sharp front teeth, stained orange by aspen bark, were made for cutting soft wood, not for gnawing at unyielding ice. Yet he kept working doggedly to free the food pile. He had partially uncovered a twig of aspen. In a few minutes he pulled it loose for her.

Eagerly she clasped it to her breast with her forepaws and swam to the house. Sculling up the tunnel, she scrambled to the mud floor and shook the water from her fur before settling down to her little feast. She nibbled slowly, to savor every scrap of bark. Ordinarily she would have turned the twig quickly in her paws, nibbling it round and round, not worrying if she left a shred of bark here or there. Now she gnawed into the clean white wood itself.

After eating, it was her habit to carry gnawed sticks to the bottom of the pond or to add them to the dam. This time she left the stripped twig for the youngsters to chew on.

Back in the pond again, she turned toward the dam, searching for something else for the young ones. A fish darted ahead of her, but she paid no attention. Even with hunger her foremost worry, she did not think of the fish as food. It was just her neighbor in the pond, probably hungry, too. Her enemies—the mountain lion, the coyote, the bear, the bobcat, the otter—had the urge to pursue and kill. But the Beaver's driving urge was to build, and to live in peace. As a vegetarian, she relished aspen bark above all, then the bark of willows and alders, the roots of water plants, and grass.

She swam along the strip of dam that showed beneath the ice, looking for edible bark on some protruding branch. She had already done this countless times, with small success, for most of the sticks and branches the beavers had woven into the dam were now old and waterlogged and had already been peeled.

The stream which fed the pond from the head of the valley in summer always carried down soil and mud during the spring runoff and after every rain. But since the forest fire, twice as much, three times as much silt as usual had collected. Into the layer of silt the Beaver now began to probe, trying to uncover some bit of food that had been overlooked. Using her forepaws as hands and her broad flat tail as a brace, she worked industriously.

Finally she succeeded in exposing a branch of spruce with bark still firm and fresh. Spruce bark did not tempt her or her family, but at least it was something to eat.

She hurried to the lodge with the branch for the young ones. Besides, it was time for her to breathe again. She could stay under water for ten minutes, sometimes a little longer, but with anxiety and hunger plaguing her, she was short of breath.

The youngsters were whimpering and wailing with hunger. Eagerly they snatched at the spruce branch, pulling off the twigs and eating the bark as avidly as young porcupines.

The Beaver returned to the food pile again to see how her mate was faring. She found him treading water, with his nose in the air space between ice and water, resting as he filled his lungs. He had managed to gnaw off a tiny end of aspen branch. It lay temptingly on the ice chips. But she would not take it—her mate must have that piece for himself. She would try elsewhere.

She turned and swam to the side of the pond where water lilies grew in summer, sending up long stems that floated flat leaves and yellow flowers. Now there was no sign of leaf or stem.

She could barely squeeze through under the thick ice.

The mud on the bottom of the pond was already furrowed where the beavers had plowed for tubers. Digging across the furrows, the Beaver finally came up with a few shriveled rootstocks. For one more day they would keep starvation away.

The yearlings and two-year-olds were quarreling over the gnawed twigs of spruce, clicking their teeth in anger, when their mother returned to the lodge. Nuzzling the yearlings to her, she murmured reassuringly and gave the rootstocks to them. How thin they were.

Tired though she was, she felt compelled to go to the pond again. This time she swam to the hole her mate had dug in his attempt to recover the flow of spring water. The water in the hole was like the rest of the water in the pond—cold and stale. Not that the Beaver minded cold water . . . her thick woolly underfur made a warm blanket, and her long, oiled guard hairs served as a raincoat. But she wanted to feel a current of warmer spring water returning to the pond.

She dug at one side of the hole to see if she could uncover

some roots. After removing a few scoops of mud, her claws grated against something hard. A large stone was imbedded in the mud just where she wanted to dig. Patiently she worked her forepaws around it and pulled it loose. Finding it too heavy to carry away, she let it fall to the bottom of the hole.

She reached into the cavity, feeling for roots that were sometimes matted around a stone. But wait! What was this? The mud seemed ever so slightly warmer where the stone had lain. She began to tear at the cavity.

In a few minutes she discovered that a thin trickle of warmer water was indeed seeping through from somewhere.

She needed air. And she needed her mate. She hurried for both.

Soon they were both digging at the hole where the stone had been—not for food this time, but for the lost spring.

Suddenly a gush of clear water swirled into the muddy pool, a gush of life-giving energy. They had tapped the seam! They had uncovered the spring at the lower level of its changed course, reinforced by underground water from the woods north of the pond. Welling up from the good earth, the water was warm and fresh compared to the stagnant pond.

Now ice would begin to melt around the food pile, slowly releasing branches and lengths of aspen trunks. The air would freshen. Even if the usual April snows came to the mountains, sealing winter in the pond for another month, the beavers would be safe!

Playfully the Beaver nibbled at her mate's cheeks, and he at hers. She churred softly in her throat. She chased him from the spring to the food pile, from the food pile to the dam, from the dam up the tunnel into the lodge.

For the first time in days she could forget about being hungry.

2

The mid-April breeze shot arrows of sunlight through the woods north of the beaver pond, bringing the unmistakable news that winter was nearing its end. A fragrance of warming needles and damp bark filled the Pine Squirrel's nostrils as he sat on a limb in his small domain at the edge of the woods. Most of the snow from the light fall of the day before had blown from the trees. Though old drifts still humped through the woods and curved around tree trunks, covering seedling spruces and imprisoning the lower branches of bigger trees, the breeze drifting down from the heights carried a hint of mellowness.

The Squirrel sensed that spring was on its way. Varnished buds on the tips of firs and spruces were beginning to swell, and willow clumps in the marsh were showing signs of life. Yet the Squirrel's buzzing chatter sounded more like scolding than rejoicing. "Chickaree, chickaree, chickaree!" he cried, twitching his tail with every chirp.

Certainly he had plenty to scold about! First, the hard winter. Although only half the normal amount of snow had fallen on the east side of the Rockies that winter, the winds had been more bitter, the cold more intense. No sooner would the Squirrel clear out his tunnels in the long drift to get at some of his buried cones, than the wind would fill the openings with snow again.

Yet weather had been only one of his worries. For some reason beyond his understanding, more squirrels than usual had come to live in his section of the forest near the beaver pond. With them had come pine martens, the squirrels' most dreaded enemy. Not that martens ever were very numerous —fierce fighting among themselves kept their numbers down —but just to see a marten bounding over the snowdrifts or dashing through the treetops paralyzed the Squirrel with fright.

Nutcrackers, too, had become more numerous. Their insolent cawing infuriated him. Several times an overbold one had even dared to swoop down and seize a cone from him as he was shucking off the scales to reach the seeds beneath.

And for the past two winters a pair of great horned owls had come to hunt in the Squirrel's part of the woods. Although they did most of their foraging at night while he slept, he had to be careful at dawn and dusk and on cloudy days.

The Squirrel, chattering on his perch in an Engelmann spruce, did not, of course, connect the increase in wildlife with the forest fire at the head of the valley two years before. He knew well enough that a fire had raged there. For days the wind had carried a bitter, biting smell of smoke and an ominous dust of ashes. For days he had waited and watched and sniffed anxiously, ready to flee if the fire came too close.

Yet it did not occur to him that wild folk from farther up the mountain were fleeing from the fire and finding refuge in his woods.

After the fire, he had ventured over a highway of treetops to look at the black desolation, the charred logs and trunks, the ruined slopes. He had come home to scold at encroaching squirrels and lurking coyotes, but his chattering stuck in his throat whenever he glimpsed a marten.

Worse than the increase in enemies, worse than the unusually cold weather, had been the loss of his mate. He really had cause for scolding about that. Yet, strangely enough, whenever he remembered his mate, he stopped chattering. An indescribable loneliness engulfed him, a loneliness too deep for sound.

As the Squirrel stretched out flat on the limb in a patch of sunlight, a great longing for his mate swept over him. He had tried to save her that day, two weeks before, when the marten came upon them chasing each other playfully through the treetops. All his mate needed was time to reach the woodpecker hole leading to the winter nest in the old limber pine. He tried to cut in, to divert the marten's attention. . . .

But the marten chose to pursue the smaller squirrel. Up and down trunks, over branches, in and out of treetops, he tore after her madly, recklessly. As fast as the squirrel and stronger, he kept gaining on her. Finally, with a desperate leap, he drove the little squirrel out of the group of trees she knew so well into unfamiliar spruces.

She raced on courageously. But there was no hope for her in trees whose branches she had not tried and tested, whose escape-places she did not know.

The Squirrel did not see the end of the chase. He heard a terrified cry, and that was all. His mate never returned.

The sunlight was warm on his back as he lay on the limb. But something about the smell of the air made him restless. In the distance one nutcracker called to another in a new spring voice. Close by, a pair of Rocky Mountain jays sported. A snowshoe rabbit, in her white winter coat with black-tipped ears, scampered along the edge of the marsh, trying playfully to elude another snowshoe. Two by two the wild folk went in spring. But the Squirrel had no mate.

He sat up and began grooming his tail. He wanted to race, to chase, to go frisking through the trees. But not alone. Was it too late to find himself another mate?

April coursed through his blood as he groomed himself. For the first time since losing his mate, his loneliness turned to eagerness.

Suddenly, with plumed tail waving, he whirled away from the safety of his home trees and headed for the deep woods. Adventure filled the air. His quivering nostrils caught it from every direction and made him daring. In his domain of fewer than a dozen trees, he knew every branch by heart—the strength of the smallest twig, the length of every leap, the merits of every hiding place. In strange trees he would have to take his chances. But suddenly he felt like taking chances!

He galloped ahead over a road of dark fragrant boughs —a high road, with mottled sunlight above and streaked and mottled shadows on the drifts below. The snow, sprinkled with short dry needles of spruces and firs, had already lost the whiteness of yesterday.

The Squirrel, like the Beaver, lived in a world without color. Green boughs, blue sky, yellow sunlight were known to him only as shades of black or white or gray. He could see the sheen and shimmer of light in the sky and on snow, sparkling on waxy needles, flashing on bird wings. On windy days gray and black shadows swayed on the forest floor; on clear bright days shafts of light pierced the forest roof. He could see varying depths of darkness when he peered from his nest at night. But colors, like the rich dark green of the branches through which he raced, and the purple-brown of tree trunks, were not of his world.

With ease he ran from one tree to the next, swerving around open places, sometimes just touching the short stiff branches of the firs, sometimes leaping a wide gap. The spruces grew longer branches, down-sweeping ones designed to slough off snow. The most wide-spreading and supple of all were the branches of limber pines, able to bend and bend without breaking under a burden of snow. From one swaying branch to the next the Squirrel dashed, sure-footed and fearless.

He was as much at home in a tree as a bird. His feet, with their long, curved, needle-sharp claws, were made for clinging to branches and tree trunks. His bushy tail served as a balancing pole when he ran along the tightrope of a branch, and as a rudder when he took a flying leap.

What a day to be alive in an evergreen forest!

Quietly and cautiously the Squirrel hurried along, his dark tail with its fringe of white-tipped hairs flowing behind him.

Silence was his best friend in strange territory. A marten's ears were as quick and sharp as his appetite for squirrels and rabbits. A bobcat's ears were as keen as his flashing, sun-flecked eyes. And why tell a peppery pine squirrel that a trespasser was coming?

Although the Squirrel belonged to the red squirrel family, he wore a coat that was rusty gray above and grayish-white beneath. It blended well with the shadowy darkness of the forest, since the fur on his back caught the brightness of the light coming from above, while his underfur remained in the shadow. When he flattened his body and tail against a high limb or sat motionless in the depths of a tree, he was almost invisible.

But his coloring gave him no protection while he was in motion. He must be constantly on guard.

A flash of movement ahead brought him to a nervous stop. Crouched on a branch, tail down, he waited. His large dark eyes, bulging out on either side of his head, gave him a surprisingly wide field of vision. Without moving his head, he could stare sidewise, upward, downward, backward, and forward—all at the same time. He seldom blinked, but his nostrils and whiskers kept twitching continuously.

Another squirrel bent on April adventures was crossing ahead of him. The Pine Squirrel waited in silence, flattened against a tree trunk. In his home trees he would chase a newcomer out of bounds, give him a fiery lecture, and warn him not to come again. But here he was content to let the stranger disappear unchallenged.

After waiting a few minutes to be sure that no enemy followed, the Squirrel darted ahead again through the shadowy forest. The breeze sporting in the high branches filled his nostrils with the fragrance of a thousand trees.

Every now and then he would jerk to a stop and sit on his haunches to listen and sniff. When he caught a squirrel scent in a tree, he would run over the trunk, his nose close to the bark, seeking out the scent posts left by other squirrels. In turn he would leave a message of his own before hurrying on.

When he felt hungry, he scampered to the top of a tree to look for cones. The trees had already been raided by squirrels and nutcrackers and wind and weather, and most of the scales on the remaining cones had opened and freed their

seeds. On the alpine firs he often found only bare spikes
of cones still standing. Yet he managed to find a few seeds
in cones on spruces and limber pines to appease his ever-
present appetite.

Soon he came to a place where a scattering of cone chips
and cores on the snow beneath a leaning tree warned him
to detour. Some squirrel's favorite eating place was a crotch
of the leaning tree! To go straight ahead would be to trespass
on another's property. But the Squirrel thought he might
find a few seeds in the midden pile, as mice and juncos did
on his pile at home.

He hesitated. He knew the owner would fight to keep
a trespasser from his homesite, just as he would fight for

his mate, his nest, his food-tree. Yet no one seemed to be around.

The Squirrel was preparing to leap for the midden pile when his sharp eyes noticed something that stopped him in his tracks. The edge of a dried mushroom was sticking out from a crevice in the bark of the leaning tree. Almost more than the nutty little seeds of cones, he relished mushrooms—fresh or dried.

With an impertinent flick of his tail, he scrambled back up the tree and along a sweeping branch. From there it was an easy jump to the leaning tree. He settled down to enjoy the mushroom.

His enjoyment was short-lived. A squirrel full of abusive language, waving his tail in a blur of rage, came charging down a nearby trunk. With a leap he rushed at the intruder who had stolen his dried mushroom.

The Pine Squirrel whirled and ran. Swirling around tree trunks, dashing, jumping, leaping, chasing, the two squirrels went, their sharp claws tearing the bark and sending showers of scales onto the already dirty snow. The outraged stranger kept up a stream of violent sputtering.

Then, as suddenly as it had started, the chase ended. The Squirrel was no longer being pursued; he must be far outside the bounds of the other's homesite. Out of breath, he crouched on a shadowy branch to rest. Next time he would make a detour around a homesite.

Carefully he licked the fur on his back and haunches and groomed his tail. He chewed the pitch from his feet where some had caught and stuck to the hairs between his toes. Licking his forepaws, he brushed them over his face. Then, with three jerks and a flick, he was on his way again.

Shadows were beginning to lengthen. As soon as the sun

went down the clammy cold of the mountain night would descend on the forest. He must find a place to sleep where he could curl up in the blanket of his tail and keep warm. Slowing down, he began to search the trees for an old bird's nest suitable for a husky four-year-old squirrel.

Soon he spotted one halfway up a tall spruce, close to the trunk. It looked big and bulky, but many larger birds built their nests on a platform of sticks and twigs, with the true nest of soft grass and moss on top.

Up the trunk he ran to look into the deserted nest. But the nest was not deserted! He found himself looking into the angry eyes of a Rocky Mountain jay. He had forgotten that the jays nested early, when the weather was still forbiddingly cold at night. Without waiting for a peck from the sharp beak, the Squirrel withdrew in haste.

Just before dusk turned into night, he found an old flicker hole in a half-dead limber pine, whose top had been broken off in a storm. The hole had been used many times before, by summer-nesting birds and by a mouse family. He could piece together its history as he sniffed around it. The empty nest suited him well, and he went to sleep, tired and hungry and lonely, with his tail curled over his nose.

Early the next morning, scratching around in the litter of the nest, he found some dusty old seeds the mice had left. He ate them with satisfaction. Usually mice stole from *him,* sniffing out his underground caches of cones at night while he slept, thrusting their narrow paws into the pockets of scales to reach the seeds. Now, for the first time, as he sat munching their old seeds, the smell of mice did not set him sputtering and fuming.

Breakfast over, his fur combed and his tail groomed, he started out again. Already he was a good distance from home. Was his quest in vain? He had seen signs of a number of squirrels, but no young females were scampering around looking for a mate.

The ground dipped suddenly to a snowy canyon patched with clumps of aspens. On the other side a jagged outcropping of rock towered over the canyon. Always curious, the Squirrel paused to look around him. He felt an urge to investigate the strange rock pile and the dwarf trees and bushes that had taken root in cracks and clefts across the way. Wind had blown much of the snow from the rocks and April sun had polished the tops of drifts to mirror brightness. Perhaps over there he could find seeds and dried berries clinging to some of the bushes. . . .

It would be dangerous, of course. But by crossing the canyon farther up, where it narrowed to a slit, and circling around behind the cliff, he would have the protection of trees most of the way. The canyon looked peaceful enough in the dazzle of early-morning sunlight. He could hear a flock of cheery chickadees in the aspens, and the sharp cries of nuthatches tagging along with them.

Just as he was about to leave for the rock pile, a whiff of wind brought an exciting scent. Waving his tail eagerly, he scampered to the tree on the edge of the canyon and sniffed up and down the trunk. A female squirrel had passed there not long before! Would she be coming back?

As he sniffed along an overhanging branch, a sudden movement in the canyon below caught his eye. A movement of white against white. He kept perfectly still, and stared.

A small white animal with a black tip on its tail was exploring the boulders at the foot of the cliff, slipping quickly along close to the ground. Now and then it stopped and rose to its hind legs to look around. Then it leaped ahead. A weasel!

Without moving a muscle the Squirrel watched tensely. A weasel was an enemy almost as much to be feared as its larger cousin, the marten.

He watched the weasel weave back and forth and climb part way up the cliff. Still in its winter coat, the little animal was hard to see against the snow. Sometimes it seemed to disappear altogether. Then it would pop up again in open places in the rocks.

The scratching sound of claws on the bark of a nearby tree distracted the Squirrel's attention. A lithe young squirrel was running toward his tree, flowing along with speed and grace. He chirred softly.

She stopped, surprised, her nose twitching in his direction. Before he had time to chirr again, a large male squirrel came whisking along on her track.

The Pine Squirrel waited quietly. If these two were already mates he would not interfere. But if this was just a one-sided chase. . . .

The little female took a step or two toward him, flicked her tail, and leaped across to his tree. She made no teasing gesture toward the other squirrel, gave no sign of interest.

The big fellow began to advance angrily, baring his teeth and scolding at the top of his voice. This would be a fight! The Squirrel barked out a fiery answer to the challenge and spread the hairs of his tail to make it look big and impressive. His whiskers bristled. With a flying leap he vaulted over his adversary and darted to the other side of the tree. A limb overhanging a canyon was no place for a fight.

Such a stream of invective as the two hurled at each

other! Such clawing, biting, and maneuvering for position. And all the time the female sat calmly on a limb, grooming her coat.

The Squirrel was getting somewhat the worst of it. His face stung from a gash in his cheek; his back hurt where sharp claws had raked his fur. And then . . . he caught a flash of something white racing toward the tree. The weasel. He had forgotten about it, forgotten that the noise of the fight would lure the weasel from the canyon. Now it was running up the tree trunk.

With a mighty effort the Pine Squirrel shook himself free and dropped to a lower branch just as the weasel whisked along the limb. The other squirrel, with his back toward the trunk, did not know what struck him when the weasel leaped and dug his sharp teeth into the scruff of his neck. There was a scramble, a tussle, a sharp cry from the squirrel as the two dropped to the snow, locked in combat.

The Squirrel did not wait to see the outcome. Waving his tail in triumph, he chirred urgently to the little female. With an answering call, she came running. Then he whirled and whisked along the green highway into the forest, showing her the way home.

The Freak Storm

1

MAY CAME, and the beavers were still locked in the pond.

The last two weeks of April had been bitterly cold, with a pale far-away sun barely able to send shimmers of light through the ice-roof of the pond. Time seemed to stand still, like the cold. No snow fell. Yet no snow or ice melted. The mountain valley still wore the look of winter.

Oblivious to weather, the beavers lived in the safety of the pond. Their fear of being trapped by the ice had left them when they uncovered the spring. The warmer water soon softened some of the ice around imprisoned branches, and vigorous chipping freed twigs on one side of the pile. For the first time in days the beavers feasted. For the first time in days they carried handfuls of peeled sticks to the bottom of the pond.

A noticeable freshness returned to the water and air of the pond, with oxygen-filled spring water bubbling in. The young beavers played again, chasing each other through canals, along the dam, and even through the narrow space under the ice where a few unclaimed water lily tubers lay waiting for spring.

On the churned-up pond bottom, where their parents

33

had grubbed for roots and tubers, the youngsters played in the soft black mud. They scooped it up with their forepaws and piled it into miniature lodges and dams, for the instinct to build was strong in them.

Yet the mother Beaver still had one cause for concern as she watched the youngsters play. One of the yearlings had not recovered from the famine as quickly as the others. He moved listlessly, often lingering in the background, avoiding the more strenuous games. Sometimes he stayed in his bed in the lodge when the others went to play. Often he whimpered in his sleep, or cried for his mother to nuzzle him.

Although time was vague in the Beaver's mind, she sensed that the melting season was close at hand. Soon the ice on the pond would crack and break under the spring sun, the stream would flow again, water would splash over the dam. Soon she would be able to take her sick yearling to the top of the beaver house to lie in the sun, while she found life-giving shoots and tender leaves for him to eat.

The Beaver knew the pattern of nature in a simple way. With the breakup of ice and the melting of snow in the valley, she and her mate would have to work to keep the dam from giving way under the tremendous pressure. But now surely nothing could happen to interfere with the easy-going life under the ice.

She was mistaken. The very next day only the whimpering of the sick yearling saved the beaver family from disaster.

Locked in as they were, the beavers had little way of knowing what went on in the world outside. Their keen sense of smell brought them no news because of the thick ice over the pond and the thick frozen roof of their house. By the end of winter their lodge smelled so strongly of beaver, they could not even catch the scent of a coyote or mountain lion standing over the clogged air vents.

Their eyes were of little help either. Except for gradations of grayness in the water of the pond during daylight hours, no light reached the beavers. The air vents in the intertwined sticks at the top of the lodge roof were too tiny to permit more than a few pinpricks of light to filter through.

Sometimes the beavers' ears brought them news of the outdoors. When an enemy clawed at the frozen roof, they listened to the muffled scratching without fear. No enemy had ever been able to break through. And even if one should, the beavers could retreat down the tunnel into the pond.

Snow fell so quietly they never knew when it came or how long it lasted. Even the roar of the wind was deadened by the thick walls of sticks and mud.

But the beavers could tell when it rained by the muted plunk! plunk! of drops on the air vents.

It began to rain before midmorning on a day in early May. During the night a chinook wind from the Pacific blew the lingering bank of cold air eastward over the plains and replaced it with spring mildness. In the wake of the chinook, a heavy mass of warm humid air settled on the mountains. Clouds opened and began to spill their burden of moisture. Instead of falling as spring snow, as it ordinarily did at that altitude, the moisture fell as rain—a slow, steady drumming of warm rain.

The Beaver, dozing in the lodge, was not disturbed by the sound of rain falling. Rain would hasten the melting of the ice. After being imprisoned in the pond for six months, she was eager to see the sun and feel its warmth soak into her fur.

Most of the day the beavers drowsed and slept with

the sound of rain in their ears. Occasionally drops worked through the roof and fell on the mud floor or plunked on the water door of the tunnel.

Content, the Beaver curled in her bed, her tail along her side. Let the rain fall! Let the ice melt! Let the sun, following the rain, draw life from the steaming earth!

But the rain was not the blessing it seemed. As the beavers drowsed, something unexpected and dangerous was happening in the valley.

Where the forest fire had robbed the slopes of trees, the rain fell on unusually deep snowdrifts between bare, windswept ridges. Without trees to hold the snow in place, the winter wind had been able to strike with full force, piling snowdrifts twenty and thirty feet deep in the hollows, and sweeping the ridges clear.

The unseasonable rain soaked into the snow of the drifts and disappeared, but on the exposed surface of frozen windswept ground it started running downhill at once. Before the fire, spruces and firs had made a thick roof of green that broke the force of falling rain. Now with the trees gone, rain fell with full force on the open slopes. With nothing to stop it, the runoff swept down to the stream bed that cut the valley.

Running down the ridges to the ice-locked stream in the valley, the rain water formed a stream of its own and went racing on top of the ice toward the beaver pond.

Here and there along the stream bed close to the pond, water-worn boulders humped above the ice. April sun had warmed the rocks, melting and cracking the ice around the edges. Into these cracks the hurrying rush of rain water found its way and began flowing under the ice as well as on top, finally gouging out an entrance into the beaver pond.

A cry from the ailing yearling roused the Beaver. She lay in her bed, listening. Rain still thumped on the roof and a quickening pit-pit of drops fell on the watery door of the tunnel. The yearling stirred and whimpered again.

Slipping from her bed on the raised circular shelf, the Beaver went to comfort him.

The minute her paws touched the mud floor she knew something was wrong. A slight slope to the tunnel door normally kept the floor well drained. Surely not enough rain had filtered through the air vents to turn the floor into soft mud.

In the darkness she felt for the tunnel opening. Her paw touched water. What had happened? Usually water in the tunnel stood several inches below the floor of the lodge. Now the tunnel was full to the top and running over, fuller than it had been even during high water of spring!

The yearling cried again, but the sound seemed far-away and unimportant now. Quickly the Beaver roused her mate before plunging into the dark water of the tunnel.

The minute she swam into the pond she could feel movement in the water, more movement than the bubbling of a dozen springs. And the water felt decidedly warmer than before. She darted toward the spring to see if it had suddenly become a gusher.

She felt the vibration of ripples as her mate dashed past her. Almost at the same moment they dove into the hole they had dug around the spring. Nothing had changed there —nothing except a strong movement of fresh water that stirred that whole side of the pond.

Propelling herself upward with the paddles of her webbed feet, the Beaver hurried to see if the ice-roof could be melting. She found that the air space had vanished! Water pressed against the solid mass of ice that covered the pond.

She did not need eyes to tell her that disaster threatened her family. She could feel by the movement of the current that water was pouring into the pond from somewhere, water that could not escape.

Her mate had headed for the bank when he left the spring. Now she hurried after him. Almost at once she was aware that she was swimming against a strong current.

She found her agitated mate at the place where the mountain stream entered the pond in summer. Rushing rain water had found a way to enter and was forcing itself into the pond, raising the water level to the ice-roof and pushing the tunnel up into the beaver house. . . .

Dashing back to the lodge for air, they found water spilling out of the tunnel, creeping toward the raised sleeping shelf. The youngsters huddled there, wailing, sensed that something had gone wrong. Because she always sought to comfort them when they were frightened or hurt, the Beaver churred to them with a reassurance she was far from feeling.

She heard her mate dive into the tunnel again. She must follow him, but the fright of the young ones made her hesitate.

She stretched to her full height and put her forepaws on the dome of the lodge. The mud, soaked by the long rain, was loosening from the sticks. But even if the beavers could tear a hole in the roof and escape before the room was flooded, where could they go? Where could they find safety?

A sudden driving impulse made her whirl and plunge into the tunnel. She must tear a hole in the dam before the beaver house was flooded!

She found her mate already at work making a hole in the dam, not at the middle where the pressure of water was greatest, but at the end near the lodge. A weak spot there would not endanger the dam when the spring breakup came.

Together they worked frantically, chewing, biting, pulling at the sticks and mud of the thick barrier that held back the water. But making a hole in the sturdy structure was not a job of a few minutes.

Meanwhile more water kept coming into the pond.

With lungs bursting for want of air, they dashed back into the lodge. Water was lapping against the sleeping shelf. They must hurry, hurry!

Before following her mate back to the dam, the Beaver delayed for a moment in order to answer the cries of her young ones. Then it suddenly occurred to her that the two-years-olds could help. More paws would be better than few. She called to them, warning the yearlings to stay on the shelf and keep out of the way.

Almost full-grown now, the two-year-olds were strong and intelligent, able to grasp the meaning of the job to be done. They followed her down the tunnel and swam after her to the dam. Soon five sets of sharp teeth and five pairs of forepaws were clawing at the mud and rocks and debris near the top of the dam.

Twice the beavers had to gnaw through a large branch. Out came the stones they had laboriously carried to strengthen the dam. Out came peeled aspen sticks and willow branches and mud and sod.

The beavers tugged and gnawed. As they made the hole deeper in the dam, one of the two-year-olds crawled in and threw mud and sticks behind him.

It would not do to make too big a hole, one that would lower the water level too drastically. Yet the hole had to be big enough to carry off the rush of rain water that kept coming in under the ice.

Finally the two-year-old succeeded in clawing out the last sticks. As he backed out of the hole, water poured through. The beavers waited, away from the suction of the hole, and listened. They could hear the splash of spray on the ice-covered rocks below the dam. They could feel the current moving past them as water escaped. Later they would block up the hole again, but now it meant life itself.

Quickly the mother Beaver turned away from the dam to hurry back to the yearlings. She pulled herself onto the muddy floor of the lodge and shook the water from her fur.

The yearlings scrambled down from the shelf to press against her.

The danger of the beaver house being flooded was over! She must take the youngsters to see the water pouring out of the hole in the dam. Still breathless from the ordeal of the narrow escape, she churred to them to follow and swam again into the strange wild pond.

2

The early-May morning before the rain found the Pine Squirrel squatting on a limb of his favorite tree, twitching his whiskers as he sniffed the air. He sensed that a change was in the offing.

He and his new mate had made the most of the unusually cold dry weather of late April. Not a flake of snow had fallen. They could not have ordered better weather for frisking and sporting through the treetops. The snowless branches offered inviting, unobstructed highways. Their sleek fur coats with woolly underfur kept out the cold. Besides, their blood ran warmer than usual in this spring of the year.

For two weeks they had raced and chased tirelessly, even investigating treetops well outside the limits of their domain.

First, of course, the Squirrel had shown his new mate the wonders and secrets of the little group of trees that made up his homestead. He took her up and down his Engelmann spruces and two alpine firs, saving the venerable old limber pine until last. This was the largest tree in his domain, growing in a rock pile at the edge of the woods and conspicuous because of its wide-spreading branches and roots wedged between boulders.

A dozen or more feet above the ground the old pine forked. One of the trunks growing out at a slight angle was so heavy with limbs it gave the tree a lopsided appearance. The other trunk, growing straight up, had been topped in a windstorm years before and was stunted and half-dead. In this trunk a woodpecker had hollowed out a nest, now the property of the Squirrel. It would make a cozy winter home and an excellent nursery.

The Squirrel showed his mate the crevices in tree crotches where a few dried mushrooms were still hidden, safe from deer and mice; the gnarly branch growing close under another where a squirrel could flatten out and be safe from attacking beak or outstretched talons; last year's summer nest, a ball of moss and bark in a spruce.

He whisked her to the ground, to the long snowdrift where six tunnels led into a maze of galleries.

Back in the trees, he showed her the long leaps, the tricky leaps; the best limbs for a sun bath; his favorite eating-place in the lopsided half of the limber pine, and the midden pile of cone cobs and scales darkening the snow beneath.

Swift-running, swift-leaping, almost birdlike in speed, they flashed through the branches, abandoning themselves to fun. They played all the games they could think of, over and over. And the magic of spring sent them frisking where they would never dare venture at a saner time of year.

Twice the Squirrel had to take measures against trespassing squirrels who acted brazenly curious about his new mate. He drove them from his territory with vigorous lunges and violent threats, his tail a blur of angry motion.

Luck had been with them when it came to enemies. The

only marten they saw was chasing a snowshoe rabbit through their domain. The only coyote was digging for mice in the marsh. Once they caught the faint scent of bobcat and ducked into the woodpecker hole for safety. They even frisked through the trees in the moonlight one night without being spotted by the horned owl.

Now the weather was changing. The Squirrel jerked farther ahead on his branch and sniffed carefully. During the night the warm wild chinook wind that roared down the mountains had driven away the cold. Snug in the old woodpecker hole, the Squirrel and his mate had heard the wind whipping through the branches, making the forest scream and moan. Trees creaked; great branches grated, groaned, and scraped against each other; dead twigs snapped, old needles skidded over the snow. The limber pine lost one of its lower branches. Then the wind died down and the air became calm again.

The Squirrel twitched his nose this way and that. The morning smelled warm and heavy, hinting of a storm abrewing. He glanced down at the long snowdrift where his tunnels ran. More snow was long overdue—April had not brought the usual heavy snows to the mountains. It might be wise to carry a few extra cones to the storage nest.

A flock of chickadees and nuthatches came chirping into the Squirrel's tree. They fell to work at once, searching the trunk and branches for insects and their eggs, pecking at crevices in the bark. They, too, seemed to sense a storm in the air and hastened to forage while they had a chance.

Chirring to his mate, the Squirrel started down the trunk, headfirst as always, stopping halfway to make sure that she was following. He heard her sharp claws digging into the bark behind him, and raced ahead. They could make a game of bringing cones to the nest. They could make a game of anything at this time of year.

The two happy-go-lucky squirrels chased each other through the tunnels of the drift before settling down to the business of finding cones. They reveled in the security of their roofed-over world. Usually being on the ground filled them with apprehension, but here in the snowdrift no enemy except a weasel could squeeze into the narrow tunnels, and weasels usually found it more profitable to hunt for mice under the snow in the marsh.

The long snowbank still covered a few storage nests of cones, a dozen or two cones in each, which the Squirrel had buried the fall before. He hid the cones carefully and well—under logs, in hollows between roots, in shallow nests beneath the needle-packed litter of the forest floor. There they dried and cured. Instinctively he knew how to place the cones, only one or two deep, to keep them well ventilated so the nourishing seeds inside would be safe from mould and spoilage.

Yet sometimes he forgot where his caches lay. In his head he carried a rough map of the places as they looked in fall, but everything looked so different under a covering of snow. Only by diligent sniffing and scratching could he find his storehouses, with his own private lick-mark on the cones.

In all, he had hidden nearly three hundred cones on his homestead. Most of them were small, coming from Engelmann spruces and alpine firs. But limber-pine cones—his favorites—were large, the largest in the forest, with smooth scales and seeds without wings.

With a new mate to show off to, the Squirrel felt on his mettle to uncover some cones.

He started a new tunnel alongside a big weathered log,

working toward the butt. He remembered that he had put some of his choicest cones under the pith of the partly hollow center of the log. As he pawed through the snow with his forefeet, he kept packing it down beneath him. His

mate came romping after him, chirring and teasing, impatient for another game of tag. But for once he refused to be diverted.

Uncovering a little blueberry bush, he found a few dried berries still clinging to it. He whickered the news to his mate and they scratched around eagerly to find other berries that had fallen and been preserved under the snow.

At the butt of the log the Squirrel dug his claws into the rotten wood and eagerly forced his way up into the hollow center. A familiar and annoying scent came to him as he scrambled into the log. Though his mate nudged him to move along, he stopped to sniff. The log reeked with the lingering smell of deer mice. Had they found his cache?

Impatiently his mate frisked past him, nipping his ear as she ran. He let her go unchallenged, and began digging under bits of pith and bark for his cones.

The first one he found carried the unmistakable smell of mice. Sitting on his haunches, he clasped the big cone in his forepaws, base up, and began nipping off the scales. The seeds were gone.

He threw down the cone and stamped angrily with his forefeet. His mate came on the run.

Together they dug out the rest of the cones. Every one had been tampered with. Irritated, they sat nibbling the few seeds they could find.

By the time the Squirrel located another cache under the snow and carried out the first cone, the storm broke. He paused at the tunnel entrance in amazement. Trees were turning dark with rain, not white from snow. Rain in the mountains so early in spring? A warm moistness filled the air that hung over the forest. Drops ticked on the branches and dripped through to the snowdrifts below.

Shaking a raindrop from his nose, the Squirrel decided not to take the cones to the storage-nest after all. Since he and his mate would weather out the rain in the woodpecker hole, it would be better to take them there. With a flourish of his tail he leaped across the drift to the limber pine. His mate, carrying a spruce cone in her mouth, came frisking after.

They made several more trips for cones before the rain settled down to a steady click-spat-drip through the branches. Then in the dry comfort of the woodpecker hole they drowsed the hours away. As late afternoon turned to dusk, they nibbled some seeds, fluffed up the dry grass and moss of their beds, rubbed noses, and settled down for the night.

All the next day rain fell steadily, bringing the gray sky down with it. Snowdrifts shrank, and rain and snow together sank into the blotter of brown litter on the forest floor. A few trickles of moisture escaped down the gentle slope to the marsh, but most of the rain and melting snow found its way toward the hidden tangle of tree roots. There was no runoff as on the fire-ruined slopes at the head of the valley.

The top of the weathered log where the deer mice had raided the Squirrel's cache began to show above the shrinking drift. The lichen-splotched head of a boulder appeared. One by one the entrance holes into the drift vanished; one by one the tunnels collapsed.

And still the rain dripped down.

On the second afternoon, the Squirrel ventured out for some pieces of mushroom hidden beneath flaps of bark on the lopsided part of the tree. Where drops had splashed on the exposed edges, the mushrooms had swollen to twice their size. The squirrels ate the mushroom pieces avidly, having exhausted their seed supply hours before. That night they went to sleep feeling hungry. The Squirrel would have to dig out more cones in the morning, no matter what the weather.

Before the first gray light of dawn showed in the round hole of the nest, the rain had stopped. The Squirrel cocked an ear to listen for the muffled sound of falling drops. All was quiet. He scrambled to the door-hole and peered out.

Darkness and quiet hugged the woods. Not a twig stirred, not a lingering drop dripped from the branches. No puffs of white on the needles or white piping along the twigs showed that the rain had turned to snow. The Squirrel thrust his head from the nest to sniff. All the warmth had gone from the air.

Jumping back to the nest, he curled up and went to sleep again.

Morning came in silence. Usually chickadees and nuthatches were out early, twitting and calling as they looked for their breakfast of tiny insect eggs or larvae under the bark. This morning only the grayish-white light beyond the nest-hole showed that night was over.

The Squirrel stirred lazily. A pang of hunger made him sit up. He must find some cones.

With a flip of his tail and a scratch of claws, he was at the door looking out. What had happened to the world? Every branch, bending and curving under a glassy burden, seemed to be encased in a strange transparent covering. What could it be? Not frost. Frost thickened the needles with spicules of white and turned the twigs into sprays of white-fringed flowers. The Squirrel sniffed as he stared.

Without warning, a mass of frigid air had moved up from the plains during the night and spread across the high valley. As the bitter cold crept through the woods, every raindrop froze solid where it fell. For two hours, three hours, raindrops turned to ice, coating the tree trunks, and arching twigs and branches into unnatural curves. When the rain stopped, the ice remained—transparent, glistening, heavy.

The Squirrel's mate barked impatiently behind him. Now that the rain was over, she wanted breakfast.

He clung to the edge of the hole, staring, sniffing, listening. Though almost four years old, he had never seen the world look just like this. Curious and hungry, he leaped for a convenient branch a short distance below the woodpecker hole.

He had made the leap dozens of times, hundreds of times. But this morning it was a mistake.

His claws failed to catch in the bark as he leaped! He felt himself skidding while he struggled to get a grip on the branch. He began to slip, to fall. . . .

Instinctively stretching his legs wide and spreading his tail like a parachute to brake the fall, he dropped twenty feet to the shrunken snow. A shower of ice crystals fell with him.

He had fallen before, but never so unexpectedly as this, and never in such a sprawling heap upon landing. Usually

he bounced back from a fall as if nothing had happened. Frisk, whisk, and he would be scampering up the trunk again. But this time he had no control of his feet—they slid in all directions on the glaze of ice.

His whole forest world was encased in ice. What could he do? Where could he go? He could not get a footing on a tree trunk to climb to safety, yet he dare not stay trembling in the open where a coyote or bobcat might spy him.

Skidding over the ice-crust on the dirty snow, he headed for the old drift. If only one of his tunnels remained, he would have a place to hide. The noise of his claws scratching on the ice echoed among the tree trunks. A sharp-eared marten could hear him a long way off!

He found the drift changed beyond recognition, shrunken into itself and entirely sealed over by ice-glaze. It offered no refuge. Not one of the tunnel entrances remained— he could not even see where they had led into the snow.

Slipping and sliding, he managed to crawl onto the log that showed above the snow. There, at least, his rusty gray coat would not stand out so conspicuously. But sharp eyes could pick him out, and he had no place to run.

Suddenly a clinking, crashing sound came from the marsh nearby. Some creature heavy enough to break through the ice-crust was out hunting for breakfast. Tensely the Squirrel listened, his feet spread wide for balance. He peered ahead through the tree trunks. A clump of willow brush blocked his view of the marsh; he could see nothing.

Crack! Crash! The sound came again through the cold clear air. He dared not crawl along the log for a better view for fear he would fall and give himself away. With his heart beating furiously, he waited. Then, just for a second, he caught a glimpse of a coyote poking through the willow shrubs. Was he on the trail of a snowshoe rabbit crouched in an ice cave, or was he looking for a grouse imprisoned in a snowbank, unable to force its way through the crust?

The Squirrel looked nervously around without moving his head, searching for a place of safety. He could hear the coyote moving noisily, breaking through the crust with every step, warning the small wild folk to beware. The Squirrel's whiskers quivered as he waited. If it came to a chase, he could skid along on top of the crust. The coyote would be slowed down by breaking through. A squirrel might wear out a coyote on an ice cover like this . . . unless another enemy cut in.

Crash! Clink! The coyote was moving toward the beaver pond, away from the Squirrel's domain. And just at that moment, poking a sleepy eye above a bank of clouds, came the sun.

Without blinking the Squirrel stared at the blaze of brightness and the vastness of clear sky above. Every twig on the willow clumps before him began to vibrate with shimmer, every icy tuft of dry grass showing above the snow glittered with icy sparks. The marsh snow was adazzle with light.

He felt like chirring with joy, but instinct made him keep silent. Soon, in the glare of the May sun, the ice would loosen on the sunny side of the old limber pine and he could get back to his nest. Breakfast could wait!

Narrow Escape

1

THE WATER of the beaver pond danced with the brightness of early-June sun. In the evergreens at the edge of the marsh, the chatter of a pine squirrel sounded faintly above the rush of the stream that brought snow water down the valley to the pond. A woodpecker drummed on a dead tree in the aspen grove. Now that oily leaves were beginning to show among scraggly catkins, the aspens made a soft gray-green cloud over the slope south of the pond. Soon tiny seeds coated with a fluff of cotton would be floating on the water.

In this wettest season of the mountain year, pockets of water sparkled among greening sod humps in the marsh. Willow shrubs were in full bloom, flaunting masses of yellow from pollen-laden catkins. The snow-covered world of winter had vanished. In its place the bursting life of spring surged around the beaver pond.

The mother Beaver and her ailing yearling lay on the roof of the lodge, soaking up the sunshine of early morning. She could not get enough of smelling the air, even the unseasonably warm air of this strange year. Winter had brought too much cold and too little snow. Spring had brought rain instead of snow, and then weeks of dryness instead of more rain. But the pond still spread itself into the marsh and the sound of its abundance was music to her ears.

Now the pond water was completely renewed, recharged with oxygen, even as the mountain world around the pond had become recharged with life.

The Beaver had made a fairly smooth sunning spot on the roof by nipping off the ends of sticks and plastering the place with mud. Healing sunlight and the vitalizing shoots she brought the young one were beginning to restore his strength.

The mother Beaver was weary after the long winter. These

days nothing appealed to her more than drowsing in the sunlight with the busy sounds of spring in her ears and its fragrance in her nostrils. She needed rest and her usual spring diet of greenery. Any day now her kits would be born.

May had been a hard month at the beaver pond.

After the two-day rain, when water gouging its way under the ice had forced the beavers to cut a hole in their dam, a sudden freeze had slowed down the force of the stream. But the ice-glaze soon melted and snow in the valley began to sink under the brilliant sun. For days not a cloud appeared in the sky, to check the melting. The valley became a dazzle of water and shrinking snow.

With the protecting trees gone at the head of the valley, the great snowdrifts, packed into draws and depressions between windswept ridges, melted too fast. Slopes ran with water hurrying to join the already swollen stream. The stream in turn dumped its burden of water and silt into the beaver pond. After the rain, everything came at once in a rush.

The Beaver and her mate had to be constantly on the alert for possible breaching of the dam. Every night during the time of fastest melting, with the help of the two-year-olds, they worked to repair the damage caused by rushing water during the day. Hour after hour they cut trees, floated logs and branches, and carried stones and sticks to strengthen weakened places in the dam. They dove to the bottom of the pond with much splashing and commotion to bring up armfuls of mud for plastering and filling.

By keeping their dam in good repair, they were unwittingly preserving the well-being of the entire valley. The dam slowed down the wild rush of the stream, preventing the valley from being eroded into ugly gullies, and keeping tons of earth and silt from being carried downstream.

Behind the dam, water spread out over the marsh and sank slowly into the soil, to raise the ground water level and supply underground reservoirs. Without the dam, the pond and marsh would disappear, and with them would go the homes and feeding grounds of many animals.

But the Beaver and her mate maintained the dam for their own safety and protection, not for the benefit of the valley. Without a dependable dam, water would drain from the pond, leaving their lodge high and dry, their tunnel open to enemies.

That enemies prowled near the pond, the Beaver was well aware. Coyotes often used the dam for a bridge, leaving their scent on sod and sticks. For hours at a time they would slink around, hoping to catch a beaver on shore. Bobcats lay in wait in the shadows when the beavers had work to do. Twice during the busy nights of reinforcing the dam, the Beaver had been frightened from her tree-cutting by the scent of a mountain lion. Twice the strong scent of a bear had warned the family to stay in the pond. On those nights they worked on the dam as well as they could, using stones and mud from the pond bottom and branches left from their storage pile.

The Beaver had never known anything like the flood of water that poured into the pond and spread over the marsh after that unexpected early-May rain. In the sunny days that followed, snow-melting days, water flowed ceaselessly over the top of the dam.

The dam, built by the Beaver's grandfather, had been kept in repair by his descendants. It had always been able to slow down the force of the spring flood by spreading water over the marsh. But this year too much water had come too quickly. The dam groaned and sagged. Yet it held.

Now, in the first week of June, water still splashed merrily over the dam but, barring a cloudburst, the danger was over. Already, because of persistent heat and dryness, the flow of the stream had slackened.

The Beaver lay blinking in the sunlight, enjoying herself. Lazily she watched a whisk of wind send fleets of silver ripples across the pond. She listened to the faint lap of water against the lodge. Lifting her nose, she sniffed the mingling odors of spring—the pungent smell of aspen bark, of earth giving up the last of its frost; the fragrance of flowering willow shrubs and wakened marsh grass and flowers. Winter had disappeared into the maze of memories that made up the Beaver's past. All that mattered was the present sparkling day.

She had seen her mate swim along one of the swollen canals into the marsh, to eat his fill of young leaves and grass. At this time of year she expected him to be restless. In a few weeks he would start off on a summer of adventuring and exploring, not to return until early September.

Before long the two-year-olds would be leaving, too. They were nearly full-grown now, vigorous and canny, old enough to be starting a life of their own. As soon as her kits were born, her mate would send the two-year-olds out to make their own way in the world. She would probably never see them again.

Affectionately she nuzzled the youngster drowsing beside her. The yearlings would be with her another year. Then they, too, would go. That was the way of life in the beaver pond—kits came and two-year-olds left; yearlings stayed without a care in the world.

A swarm of mosquitoes buzzed around her head, settling on her nose and ears. Impatiently, the Beaver rubbed her head with her forepaws. Sometimes a sun bath was not worth the annoyance of mosquitoes!

Now thoroughly roused, she began to groom herself. First she ran the long claws of her forefeet through her fur to give herself a good scratching, then she combed her coat with her hind feet. Each webbed hind foot had a combing-toe with a split nail which could reach nearly every part of her body.

Like all beavers, she took pride in keeping her coat clean and sleek. When she finished her combing, she oiled her outer guard hairs with waterproofing from the oil-glands under her tail. She noticed that her underfur was thinning, even coming out in little bunches . . . a sure sign of warmer weather on the way.

Noisy splashing near the dam told her that the two-year-olds had come out to play. She watched lazily, their figures dim to her nearsighted eyes. One youngster would try to scramble to the top of the dam, the others rushing to pull him down. Then each in turn would hurry to another place and try to scramble up without being caught.

The puny yearling at her side was whimpering. He had had enough sunlight. She nudged him awake and churred to him to follow her into the lodge to finish his nap.

Soon she was back on the roof alone. She saw one of the two-year-olds swim away from the dam and hoped he would not come to bother her. But he came, sculling straight for the beaver house. In a moment he began to scramble to the roof.

Curling her lips, she showed the full length of her orange-colored cutting teeth. Though she rarely snarled, a low threatening noise now warned her son to keep away. She wanted to be alone.

He hesitated, surprised at her bad temper. Then he took another step forward. She lunged at him. In consternation, he dove back into the pond and raced to rejoin the others at the dam.

She settled back to her privacy, almost as surprised as the youngster at her outburst of temper.

Her mate came swimming into the pond from the marsh and she watched to see where he was going. He swam slowly, carrying something heavy against his chest. Another stone, perhaps, to strengthen the dam. He would not leave for his summer wanderings until he was sure that the dam was safe and sound. Down went his head and up swung his rump as he dove with his load. In a few minutes he came up empty-handed and swam to the marsh again.

A stir of breeze bringing the smell of growing things reminded the Beaver that she was hungry. She had eaten little that morning in her zeal to feed the yearling. Although dawn and dusk were her usual feeding times, she would go ashore now for some marigold leaves and young sedges. . . .

Rising on her haunches, forepaws clasped to her breast, she tested the air by sniffing and turning her head from one side to the other. All seemed peaceful at the pond. Across the marsh came the scolding chatter of a squirrel, a common enough sound. Two crows cawed over the pond. Now that the summer birds were back, morning was loud with calls and singing.

She looked toward the bank where short grass grew sweet and tender. June always began a new rhythm in her life.

Her appetite for aspen bark left her and she craved grass, shoots, and bursting buds.

Satisfied that no enemies lurked within sight or scent, she slid into the water. She swam slowly, only the top of her head out of water with eyes, ears, and nose showing. Paddling with her webbed feet, moving them alternately underwater, she barely disturbed the smoothness of the pond.

Before climbing ashore she made her usual pretense of changing her mind and turning back. To draw out enemies who might be watching, she swung around and headed again for the beaver house, her eyes wide open, her nostrils twitching. Nothing happened, so she sculled back toward shore.

In a moment she was pulling herself onto the marshy bank and shaking the water from her fur. From habit she sat on her haunches to test the air once more before burying her nose in the fragrance of spring growth. Head high, nostrils twitching, she sniffed. Nothing warned her of danger. The downwind carried only the scent of what lay higher up the valley. What might be below her, she had no way of knowing.

Some marigolds grew near a log half-sunken in the mud. She moved ahead to nip at them. Her hind feet were longer and more powerful than her forefeet, and she walked clumsily, bearing most of her weight on her webbed hind feet. The rich black soil of the marsh oozed with moisture from deep frost working itself out, making walking even more difficult. As she waddled along, her leathery tail left a broad muddy track between her footprints.

Her safety lay in alertness and in keeping close to the pond. None of her enemies in the high valley would follow her into the water. Of course, if otters should come, she would not be safe either in the pond or in the lodge, but so far no otters had invaded her domain.

Walking with her nose close to the ground, she smelled the musky trail of a shrew, but saw no sign of it. She crossed a mouse path skirting the log. Marigold leaves and clumps of nearby grass tasted good and whetted her appetite for more. She scrambled over the log and rose high on her hind feet to reach a twig of alder shrub with tiny leaves just breaking from bud sheaths.

At that moment a sudden upswirl of wind brought her the terrifying scent of a coyote!

Her one impulse was to reach the pond as quickly as possible. But before she could get a good start, a dark form leaped from behind a willow clump and sprang toward her.

The coyote had been waiting downwind, on the slim chance that the Beaver would come ashore.

Scudding for the bank as fast as her clumsy legs would carry her, she headed straight for a patch of oozy mud instead of swerving to seek firmer ground. She relied on her webbed feet to come to her rescue. They would give her footing a broad base and keep her from sinking.

She heard a swash in the mud behind her, followed by a sharp bark of rage. The coyote had slipped. His misfortune gave her precious seconds to scramble ahead.

He was on his feet again, squishing through the ooze. His scent, strong upon her, urged her to frantic haste.

The pond lay just ahead. In a final burst of energy, the terrified Beaver dove into the water, whacking her tail to warn the others. The coyote's teeth snapped the empty air behind her.

The smooth, soothing touch of water engulfed her, surrounding her with protective arms.

Quickly she swam underwater to the middle of the pond, then surfaced to venture a look. A muddy, bedraggled coyote stood on the shore, glaring at the water.

She dove with scarcely a ripple and hurried to the beaver house. She was safe! She was home again!

A little later her kittens were born. There were only two of them this time, after the hard winter—two fuzzy little kits with tiny flat rubbery tails, sharp points of teeth, and wide-open black eyes.

She nuzzled them in the fresh bed she had made for them, and nestled down. The days of hunger were over, the days of ice and flood and hard work. She was safe from the coyote. The only thing that mattered now was this new life beside her.

2

Now that the month of longest days and shortest nights had come, the Pine Squirrel had more time on his hands than usual. He busied himself around his domain, fussed and scolded on the slightest provocation, and occasionally went adventuring beyond his boundaries with curiosity or mischief in his eye.

But lately everything had been going wrong! Looking down from his perch in the forked spruce that early-June morning, he stamped his forefeet impatiently.

A few days before, the happy hours of playing with his new mate had suddenly come to an end. Now she was spending all her time in the old woodpecker hole in the limber pine with a family of blind, naked, squirming, hungry young ones. For three more weeks they would be blind and helpless; for longer than that their mother would have to nurse them. He would be left alone.

As a father, he had certain duties, but he was not overly conscientious. He must constantly be on the alert to keep intruders from coming into his trees and finding the nest. He must fight, if necessary, to protect his family. Yet he himself must never go near the young ones. If he did, his mate would drive him off.

It irritated him to see her getting along so well without him. The few times a day she hurried off to eat or drink, she scarcely noticed him. The same thing had happened with his old mate last year and the year before. How upsetting a family was! More than once he went off in a huff, forgetting his duties as sentinel.

In mid-May he had helped clean out the woodpecker

hole as part of the sport with his new mate. They had thrown out an accumulation of shredded bark, moss, grass, and cone shucks. But when it came to making a fresh bed, his mate insisted on doing it herself. For a whole day he sulked, impatient to sport with her again. Then he set about repairing his last summer's nest high in the bushy top of a spruce. He would need it, with warm weather coming so early.

Because of the light snowfall during the winter, his last year's ball of a nest had survived in good condition. The platform of sticks on which it rested was still sturdy. The nest itself still kept out water and wind, although some of the shredded bark on the outside needed renewing. Besides, his door flap had to be refashioned, and he needed new tree moss for his bed.

After the nests were ready, he and his mate had time to play again in the treetops. Then, four days ago, the babies had been born. He no longer was first in his mate's eyes.

On top of family troubles, the weather had been annoying. After the early rain the month before and the sudden ice-glaze over every twig and branch in the woods, the sun had shone too feverishly for so early in the year. The dry heat continued into June. Still in the process of changing from his heavy dark winter fur to his lightweight summer coat, the Squirrel was often uncomfortably hot.

His forefathers had chosen to live in cool mountain forests where summer came late and left early. This year something had gone wrong with the timetable. Summer had come too soon.

Snowdrifts vanished with surprising swiftness. Usually they kept the air cool under the roof of branches until well into July. This year, because of the light snowpack and early rain, hardly a drift showed in the woods in early June.

The low blueberry bushes bloomed early, with flowers like tiny bells, before the leaves were fully out. Even the Engelmann spruces and alpine firs flowered ahead of time, their tops thick with bloom. Buds on the pines elongated early to form "candles"—out of which would come the year's new needles. Light green tips decorated the twig ends of dark firs and spruces.

This would be another warm, dry day. As the Squirrel surveyed his world from a high limb, a swarm of gnats zizzed through the branches to hover around his head. Their thin, high-pitched zizzing infuriated him, and the persistent way they had of getting into his eyes and ears. They were always a torment in spring and early summer. He lashed his tail and struck at them with his forepaws. Ducking his head, he closed his eyes and rubbed his ears.

Suddenly he spun around and raced down the tree like a whirlwind, leaving his tormentors caught in the branches.

For a few minutes he clung to the trunk several feet above the ground, head raised, whiskers twitching, feet wide apart. Was it safe to jump down? He had nibbled only a few buds early that morning because he had seen a hawk swinging over the marsh. Now he was hungry. Some cones probably still lay hidden in his storehouses, if he could find them.

Satisfied that no enemy prowled nearby, he leaped down and began to sniff over the matted needles between leafing blueberry bushes in a search for cones. At the same time his nose brought him news of recent happenings on the forest floor. A chipmunk had been scratching at his midden pile. Two mice had chased each other around the hollow log.

In many places the thick debris was pocked with holes he had dug in his winter search for cones. He was unaware of his worth as a forester. It did not occur to him that his digging aerated the ground and opened ways for melting snow and rain to sink quickly to the wide-spreading root systems of the trees. Nor did he realize that his instinct to store cones in the ground assured the growth of seedlings. Some of the lost seeds would sprout and grow into trees—to take the place of those blown down by wind or destroyed by beetles, drought, fire, or lightning.

He sniffed his way to a spot between the partly exposed roots of the limber pine wedged in an outcropping of stone. There, digging under a loose mat of needles, he unearthed first one cone, then another. Seizing one in his mouth, he scampered to the top of the log and began to snip off the scales to get at the seeds.

The first seed he rejected as being too dried and shriveled. The second he ate without enthusiasm, detecting a slightly musty flavor. The third had lost its nuttiness because it was swelling, getting ready to sprout. Disgusted, he threw down the cone.

What he wanted was something fresh and juicy, not seeds from last year's cones! Now that other food was growing in the woods and along the marsh, he could afford to be fussy about the taste of seeds. He looked around cautiously. Except for the busyness of birds nearby and far away, all seemed quiet. From the forest a pair of ruby-crowned kinglets called to each other: "Tee tee tee too too too, tee-diddle, tee-diddle, tee-diddle." A woodpecker drummed from the direction of the beaver pond.

The Squirrel decided to venture into the marsh for bursting buds and tender bark of willow twigs, a flower head or two, perhaps a big beetle. Later he might slip into the trees beyond his boundaries to see if he could steal a bird's egg.

He darted down the log, pausing at the end to sniff and listen again. Going into the marsh away from his well-known trees meant taking a risk. Some of his enemies liked to prowl among the willow brush, looking for mice and voles and rabbits. Besides, out there in the open marsh he was vulnerable to attack from above—from a sharp-eyed hawk, or one of the black ravens that summered in the mountains.

Still, the lure of fresh spring food urged him on. He could outrun most of his enemies in a short race for a tree, if he did not allow himself to be surprised. And caution was bred into his very bones.

He moved ahead with jerky leaps and pauses toward his favorite clump of willow shrubs near the marsh edge. This morning, with an alert eye on the willows, he stopped to eat the first two opening buds of a golden banner plant. Then he bounded ahead with vigorous leaps that brought his back feet in front of the print of his forefeet.

A half-buried log ran into the bushes where the Squirrel liked to stand to reach the twigs. With his forepaws he pulled down supple little branches and held them while he chewed at the spring sweetness.

Quietly he slipped down the log like a whisk of shadow, glad to be in the shade again. A marsh open to the bright eye of the sun did not appeal to him. Reaching for a tender shoot, he was just beginning to enjoy his first bite when something ahead caught his attention. He stopped chewing. Ever curious, he craned his neck forward. Something dark and bushy was moving up and down, up and down, in a clump of willows just breaking into leaf.

What could it be? The breeze out of the west was barely strong enough to shake pollen from the branches. Yet something was definitely moving up and down, as if swung by a heavy wind.

He relaxed his hold on the twig and moved stealthily to the end of the log. Still under the protection of branches, he felt safe. He peered through the slender branches, moving his nose to catch a scent. No scent reached him. Although he could see quite well from his new position, he still could not figure out the strange up-and-down movement.

His were not the only curious eyes in the marsh. He saw a snowshoe rabbit moving with cautious hops from beneath a nearby clump of brush where it had been hiding. It stopped not far away to stare at the movement ahead. Its ears were no longer white tipped with black, and its fur coat had lost the glistening whiteness that blended so well with winter snow. Now its darker color melted into shadowy summer places.

As the Squirrel watched out of one eye, the hare hopped ahead again.

Suddenly a coyote who had been moving his tail in the willows to trick some curious creature into the open, swung around with a swirl and a swish and leaped toward the rabbit sound!

The watching Squirrel trembled. Another step or two and he would have betrayed himself, all to satisfy his curiosity. He could hear the snowshoe rabbit racing across the marsh with the coyote in pursuit.

Whisking back down the log, out of the willows, across the open stretch of marsh, the frightened Squirrel reached his own domain. He raced up the first tree trunk and, squatting safely on a limb, screamed defiance at the tricky coyote. The noisy scolding drifted over the marsh to the beaver pond.

From his perch he could not see whether the hare escaped the coyote. But he warned anyone who cared to listen that an enemy was abroad, a sly, clever enemy who had cheated an innocent squirrel out of his breakfast.

Breakfast! Where was he going to get anything to eat now? The coyote had spoiled the willow clump for him—for today, at least. Would he have to go back to his cache of old cones? If only he knew where a kinglet or chickadee or pine siskin had its nest! An egg or a fledging would be a welcome change indeed.

Out of one eye he saw his mate poke her head from the woodpecker hole and look around. She listened and twitched her whiskers for a moment, then ducked back to her babies.

He stopped chattering when he heard the long-crested jays. They lived north of his domain in the tall pine with a lightning gash down its trunk. On one of his adventures he had discovered their nest, a carelessly-put-together affair of sticks and twigs, high in a crotch. He was careful to watch quietly from a nearby tree, afraid of rousing their wrath by going too close. Long-crested jays lost no more love on him than he lost on them.

Why were the jays screaming at the top of their voices? The Squirrel ran to his northmost tree to investigate. He could see the top of the jays' tree, but the sound was coming from farther away. They must have discovered an enemy. Hardly the coyote. For all his clever ways, he could not climb a tree. What enemy, then?

As he strained to look and listen, the sudden whack of a beaver's tail sounded on the pond, a warning that often floated across the marsh to the woods.

The jays still screamed. Impelled by something beside curiosity, the Squirrel ran swiftly to the end of the limb and leaped lightly to the next tree, then on to the next. A little plot was forming in his mind. He was hungry. The jays' eggs must have hatched; otherwise the birds would hardly both be away from the nest at the same time. A young fledgling, especially the fledgling of a long-crested jay, would be a most welcome prize! And what would prevent a hungry squirrel from slipping into their nest while the parents badgered an enemy?

Quickly, quietly, he hurried ahead.

As he neared the jays' tree, he paused to peer cautiously from behind a trunk. Beyond, he caught the movement of angry wings beating at something on a broken limb. A smaller bird, probably a robin, had joined the jays and was battling, too. The Squirrel could not make out the enemy but he had a good idea who it was. Meanwhile the nest lay unprotected. . . .

Rather than take the chance of having his movement discovered in the treetops, he scampered to the ground and ducked along to the base of the pine with the lightning gash. So far, so good. The jays kept screeching. Furtively he ran up the trunk.

Halfway up, through a gap in the branches, he could see the cause of the disturbance. The jays had discovered a horned owl roosting in a tree too close to their nest. In a tantrum of rage and fright, they swooped close to the owl's head, berating him furiously and trying to drive him away. Their long black crests stood straight up in anger, their dark wings flashed silver as they caught the sunlight.

At that moment the owl rose large and silent from his perch and spread his broad wings. He flew off toward the shadows of the deeper woods, with the jays and robin scolding after him.

Now! The Squirrel knew that he would have to act fast, before the jays returned. Whisk! He went scurrying toward the nest. Hurry! He swung to the bulky uneven framework of sticks and twigs cemented with mud and looked into the nest. Five scrawny little jays lay sleeping, huddled together.

But just as he was about to seize one of the fledglings with his sharp teeth, the Squirrel heard the cry of a returning jay. He hesitated. Would he have a chance to escape through the treetops encumbered by an awkward fledgling? With a jerk and flick of his tail he raced off without his prize—a second too late. The jay saw him and gave chase.

All the fury vented on the owl was now directed against the Squirrel. His safety lay in flight. If he tried to fight back, he would run the risk of having an eye put out by a sharp black beak. Twisting through the trees, he kept to the denser foliage.

With lightning darts the jay lunged toward him, trying to batter him with wings and bill. Every time he leaped for the next tree, the jay would swoop down and all but throw him off balance. And then, to add to his troubles, the second jay joined in the pursuit.

Swish! Whisk! As the Squirrel spiraled around a trunk, he felt the end of a jay's wing strike him across the back. Other wings beat above his head. The Squirrel began to wonder if he could reach his covered nest in time, or the two close limbs between which he could crawl for safety.

He shook the jays from his trail for a moment by hiding in the bushy top of a fir. Then with daring leaps he bounded toward home. Well ahead of the jays, he reached his nest and slipped through the hanging door-flap. There in the darkness of his little room, six inches across and four inches high in the center, he sat listening intently.

The jays were still scolding nearby, still searching for him. But he had eluded them.

Hot and tired, his heart pounding, the Squirrel waited. Soon he could tell from the sound that the jays had given up the search. Curling his tail around him, he slumped down for a nap.

The Shrinking Pond

1

THE WHITE, gray, and black world of the Beaver moved and breathed and changed with the passing months. In early July, during long sunny days, the pond was alive with sparkle and flutter and drifting shadows of clouds. At night twinkling reflections of moon and stars livened the dark water.

Usually summer meant leisure and fun for the beavers. With a plentiful supply of food close at hand, the dam in repair, the pond freshened, the beaver house better ventilated, days ordinarily drowsed themselves away and nights brought refreshing coolness for sporting in the water and feasting on succulent growing things. But this year, before July was half over, the Beaver already had enough of summer.

The season was not following its normal pattern.

In other years, afternoon rains and the ever-flowing stream had kept the pond full and the water from getting too warm. Deep places near the dam gave cooling relief from the shimmering brightness outside. But this year June had been unseasonably hot and dry from beginning to end. Only a few teasing sprinkles of rain fell. A thirsty wind kept sipping, sipping from the pond.

July brought little relief. Although afternoons often clouded over, and thunder rolled along the peaks, not enough rain fell on the mountain valley to water the grass and flowers. A promise, a shadow, and the sun would blaze forth again.

On top of the heat and dryness, the beaver pond was beginning to feel the effects of the forest fire. With the destruction of the great semicircle of forest at the head of the valley, no trees caught the wind and cooled it in their shade before it reached the pond. Hot dry winds that had already lost their moisture on the other side of the continental divide now swept over the pond, carrying off precious moisture.

With no absorbent litter on the slopes near timber line to conserve the little rain that fell, no moisture seeped down to renew the source of the beavers' spring.

In mid-July the stream, after having poured so much water into the pond during the time of melting drifts, ran shallow and quiet. It was now fed only by a few springs and melting snow from high in the mountains, where patches of white still lingered in hollows or clung between ridges.

By the time the shrinking stream reached the pond, it had lost some of its coolness. Worse still, not enough water flowed into the pond to make up for the loss by evaporation every day the sun beat down. Slowly and steadily the water level kept dropping.

The Beaver was beginning to feel concern for the safety of the kits and yearlings. She carried full responsibility for the family now. The two-year-olds had dropped out of her life the day the kits were born. Two weeks later her mate had left on his annual summer adventures somewhere downstream. She had no idea where he went nor when he would return, but she knew in a vague way that he would be back in time to begin preparations for winter.

The four yearlings were still part of her family. Half-grown by now, they caused her little trouble. Yet she had to keep an eye on them. They were mischievously curious, occasionally sporting in water too shallow for safety, or playing close to the bank where the paw of an enemy hiding in the willow brush might strike at them.

Though the ailing yearling had gained strength, he was still smaller and weaker than the others. Strongly attached to his mother, he often got in her way when she was trying to deepen a canal or float aspen branches home to supplement the drying grass.

Both kits, now six weeks old, were growing fast. For two weeks they had been eating solid food, yet they were not completely weaned. They were bright-eyed youngsters, quick to learn. She had them out in the water, riding them on her back and teaching them to swim when they were only two weeks old. Soon they were paddling along by themselves, their flat little tails stretched out behind them. Their ear valves and nose valves closed of their own accord to keep out the water, but she had to show them how to close their lips behind their long front teeth to keep water out of their mouths.

For her youngsters' sakes she regretted the hot dry summer. Young ones should be full of joy and play. Many nights when the yearlings and kits should have been sporting in the pond, they were listless because the air was without its usual mountain coolness.

On this July day, late in the afternoon, the Beaver ventured forth for a survey of the pond. Although the valley lay in temporary shadow, the air hung heavy and hot over everything. Usually she waited until almost dusk to reconnoiter, but today she had something on her mind: Would the beaver house be safe much longer?

She swam slowly and quietly, with only the top of her head showing above the water, grateful that the sun was not pouring down its yellow fire. From the marsh and the aspen grove came the chirping of birds, blending with the buzzing of flies and zizzing of myriads of other insects that thrived on hot weather.

Instead of swimming first to the dam, as was her custom when making a tour of the pond, the Beaver went immediately to the narrowing channel between the beaver house and the bank. A great boulder in mid-channel was emerging as the pond shrank. Another inch and its head would show above water. Then, with two easy leaps, a bobcat could jump from bank to boulder, from boulder to beaver lodge.

The beavers had not repaired the roof of the lodge after the May rain washed much of the mud plastering loose. They were glad to have more vent holes open for summer, even though the lodge could be broken into more easily. But what enemy would trouble to break into a beaver house in summer when there were easier ways of getting food elsewhere?

What really worried the Beaver was the growing danger to the tunnel. The drop of a few more inches in water level would expose its underwater entrance. Then her family's safety would be threatened indeed. If the drought continued, an enemy could soon enter the lodge through the exposed top of the tunnel.

Tonight was the night to move her family, the Beaver decided. At best, the low-roofed lodge, standing in the open in the pond, was unpleasantly hot in summer. This year's sun had turned it into an oven. Besides, it should be abandoned for a while to rid it of parasites.

Yes, tonight was the time. And tonight she would finish weaning her kits.

She swung around the pond to take a look at the old burrow that had been abandoned for almost a year. She would clean it and get it ready under the cover of darkness. It had been dug into the high bank not far from the dam, on the south side of the pond near the aspen grove where the water was still fairly deep. Shaded by a clump of willow brush during part of the day, the den would be cooler than the lodge.

As she passed the scraggly patch of water lilies, she nipped off a belated bud. The beavers had missed a few water lily rootstocks in grubbing for food under the ice-roof, but the plants were not doing well. Because of the heat, buds dried before fully opening.

The same thing was happening to flowers and grasses on the bank. They were drying before reaching maturity. Little of the usual July lushness remained in the burnished marsh, where the water table had fallen below the seeking roots of many plants.

Just as the Beaver was about to dive to the tunnel entrance leading to the burrow, she heard a small splash near the lodge. Always on the alert, she turned to look. Some small creature had jumped into the pond and was swimming frantically toward the beaver house. One of those bushy-tailed squirrels that chattered so much and occasionally got chased across the marsh!

She lay in the water, quietly watching. The squirrel was scrambling to the roof, scurrying to the other side. Shaking himself nervously, he crouched beneath projecting sticks.

Then the Beaver saw the cause of his fright. On the bank another animal had appeared, much larger than the squirrel. His eyes were straining over the water, fixed on the beaver house. A pine marten!

The squirrel crouched under the sticks in silence. The marten, reluctant to get his feet wet, ran snarling up and down the bank. Then he leaned over the pond and gingerly thrust a paw toward the water. Suddenly he drew back and cocked his head. With a quick jerk he whirled around and dashed toward the nearest willow shrubs. A thud and a squeak told the Beaver that he had caught a mouse.

The squirrel still crouched on the roof.

Diving, the Beaver swam up the short tunnel into the old den to see what needed to be done to make it livable again. The squirrel was still waiting when she returned to the pond.

As she headed for the dam, a splash told her that her visitor was leaving. He was too small for her to see from so far away. With luck he would be able to cross the marsh, through humpy sod and dry potholes, and find safety in the woods beyond. She listened curiously. Only the jangle of insects reached her ears.

With dusk coming on, the marsh became a blend of shadows and the pond turned silver-gray. All seemed well. As the Beaver swam past the aspen shore toward the drying canal, she saw sharp footprints in the mud where deer had come to drink. A lopsided white moon already showed in the sky, but it was too far away for her eyes to see.

Before fetching her young ones from the lodge, she had cleared some of the litter from the old den. It was easier than it would be with the kits tagging after her, getting in the way. Later she would bring grass and shreds of bark into the burrow for their beds.

By the time she swam to the lodge to give her youngsters the all-clear signal, sunset colors, translated into various shades of gray by the Beaver's eyes, hung over the valley. A nutcracker cawed harshly from the woods. A robin called from the aspens. Nighthawks dove out of the sky to twang over the marsh.

Her youngsters were waiting restlessly for her to come. At once the yearlings swam off toward the dam. The Beaver steered her kits to the roof of the lodge. Tonight she would not allow them to nurse. They could comb their fur while she fetched something to eat.

Holding her forepaws against her chest and propelling herself with her webbed feet, she swam toward a bank of willow brush, along the only canal that still held enough water for swimming. She was beginning to have an appetite for bark again. The heat had squeezed all the juice from grass and flower stalks, burned the sedge, wilted the lilies. Without rain no mushrooms had poked up around the logs where they usually grew. But bark was always juicy. . . .

She hesitated. Getting the leafy branches would take only a few minutes but she disliked leaving her kits alone on top of the beaver house. She questioned how quickly they would react to danger.

Hearing a sound in the aspen grove, she swung her head to sniff and caught a reassuring scent. Mule deer browsing in the grove always gave her a sense of security. Gentle and peaceful, they caused no trouble, and thumped a warning signal by bounding away if a coyote or mountain lion appeared.

The Beaver reached up to cut her willow branches.

When she returned with a load of branches held firmly in her teeth, darkness had settled over the valley. The moon had suddenly brightened to send a shimmering path across the water. She paused at the mouth of the canal to see what the yearlings were up to. Two by two they were wrestling on the dam, silhouetted against the sky.

Arms around each other, cheeks touching, bodies swaying and twisting, the yearlings were trying to knock each other off balance, a favorite sport of theirs. One pair, evenly matched in strength and size, wrestled without falling. But the undersized yearling of the other pair kept losing his balance, only to scramble pluckily to his feet again with a little cry.

As the Beaver started to swim toward the lodge, she saw a sudden dark shadow moving across the pond. She wasted no time investigating. A strange shadow meant that she must warn her young ones to dive out of sight at once. Whack! went the flat surface of her tail on the water.

She was not concerned about the yearlings—they would heed the warning without hesitation. But the kits? Dropping her load of branches, she swam ahead at full speed.

Just as she reached the beaver house, a large horned owl, with curved talons outstretched, swooped to seize a kit scrambling down the roof toward the water.

The Beaver flung herself on the roof, hissing and snarling. Her unexpected appearance startled the owl and it swerved just enough to miss its prey. Without a sound it floated up into the sky again. That was the terrifying thing about an owl—it came and went on soundless wings.

More than once in her life the Beaver had been alarmed by the sudden, silent appearance of an owl. Once she had lost a kit, tagging ashore after her, when an owl pounced out of the night sky. Often she heard the squeal of mice and the frightened cry of rabbits in the marsh when an owl was hunting.

Now she herded her youngsters into the lodge and left to retrieve the branches floating near the mouth of the canal. The moon was even brighter now, sending its light sparkling across the pond. On such a night the whole valley was alert with the activity of the hungry and the hunted. On such a night beavers must be almost as cautious as by day.

Tonight they would eat in the beaver house for the last time. She would finish her work at the burrow and move her family there. Enemies seemed to be closing in: the heat, the

shrinking pond, the drying up of the underground spring, the lurking coyote, and now the horned owl. How would she be able to get her family safely through the summer?

2

Looking down from his perch in his shadiest spruce that mid-July afternoon, the Squirrel saw a strange shadow moving toward a patch of juniper behind a log. He felt too lazy to scold, too baffled to move. The small shadow so perfectly matched the mottled and marbled darkness of the forest floor that it became practically invisible when it stopped moving.

Suddenly it reached up to snap at an insect—and gave away its identity. A dusky spruce-grouse cock was crossing the Squirrel's domain. He knew it must be a cock because in early summer a hen grouse would be followed by a number of young ones, each a tiny shadow in itself.

Let the grouse stay awhile and catch some flies! Now that the mosquitoes were thinning out, flies buzzed around in irritating numbers, pestering the Squirrel, adding to the discomfort of the dry summer.

The grouse vanished into nothingness when a small band of mule deer—some growing antlers, some growing spikes —came browsing along the edge of the woods, seeking shade. Willing to let them pass unchallenged, the Squirrel watched in silence.

But the deer had no intention of moving on. Two of them settled down on the shady side of the limber pine to chew their cuds. The largest buck reached for moss growing on the scraggly lower branches of the very Engelmann spruce in which the Squirrel perched. That called for a loud protest.

The Squirrel thumped angrily with his forepaws and vibrated his tail when two young deer, sweeping their rumps with their heads to brush off flies, stamped on the only blueberry plants that showed any sign of producing fruit. They could take their flies and go elsewhere!

For some minutes the Squirrel kept scolding, jerking part way down the trunk, barking with each jerk. He wanted the deer to know it was *his* moss they had stolen, *his* blueberry plants they had trampled. His eyes glared, his whiskers bristled. But the deer kept chewing unconcernedly, brushing flies from their thin summer coats and twitching their long ears.

The Squirrel's petulance brought his mate out of the woodpecker hole. For a moment she watched alertly from a branch of the pine. Then she scampered back to the nest to call her young ones out for a lesson.

The Squirrel was not surprised. Deer were friendly folk, coming and going without making trouble, except for the food they ate. They brought a certain amount of reassurance that all was well. An enemy like a pine marten or bobcat would hardly rush through their midst to climb a tree after a squirrel. And if anything moved, deer would see it instantly and give warning.

Whiskers still bristling, the Squirrel made another feeble protest. He remembered a time when deer had stolen some of the precious mushrooms he was waiting to harvest, and another time when they had nipped off some of his blueberries. But in this dry summer blueberries were small and shriveled . . . and where were there mushrooms to steal? Not for days had he been able to find a mushroom, though he searched and sniffed beyond the limits of his home-stead.

The absence of mushrooms and other fungi annoyed him. Always he cut and dried as many kinds as he could find and stored them in a dry place, to supplement his diet of cone seeds in winter. He usually began his harvest in July. But not this July!

He saw his mate leading the young ones to a limb for a lesson in climbing and jumping. Usually she kept them under cover during the heat of the afternoon, but with the mule deer so close she seemed to feel that the added security more than offset the heat.

Although he had little to do with them, the Squirrel felt a certain pride in the young ones, now going on seven weeks old. Their coats had furred in and their tails had already become quite bushy. For several weeks their eyes had been open to the wonders of the world of firs and spruces and pines. They already acted at home in a tree, their sharp little claws catching in the bark and holding fast whether they went up or down a trunk or scurried along a branch.

One youngster, a little larger than the others, seemed especially strong and bold. He climbed faster and ventured farther, as if consumed with curiosity to see how far he could go and what he would find. Time and again he rebelled against his mother's discipline. Instead of imitating her, he persisted in doing things his own way.

As his father watched from his quiet perch, the adventurous one left the others and scrambled to a branch of his own. His mother scolded and called, to no avail. Finally she had to go after him and drive him back, giving him a little nip on the rump for her pains.

In and out among the branches and up the trunk the

Squirrel's mate led the youngsters, urging them over difficult places with chirps and chirrs, to teach them how to use their tails for balance.

Now she was urging them to make a short jump from one solid branch to another. The precocious one did it immediately, then chafed because he was forbidden to jump farther. The others, more deliberate and obedient, were slower to learn the lesson, but received more praise from their mother. The aggressive one tried his mother's patience.

Squatting on his warm but shady branch, the Squirrel followed the lesson with interest. The young ones were learning fast. The faster, the better, as far as he was concerned! Then his mate would soon have time to pay atten-

tion to him again. He missed having her with him, even though the weather had been too hot for much frisking and chasing.

With surprise he saw her leading the youngsters down the trunk, down to the very ground. Weren't they a bit young to try scampering over matted needles? Their feet were made for clinging to bark, not for walking on uneven ground. They would be awkward and uncertain.

Two of the spike bucks stopped chewing to watch curiously. The antlered bucks paid little attention as the procession of baby squirrels reached the ground.

At the bottom of the tree a few of the cones abandoned by the Squirrel the month before still lay buried between the stones. These old cones his mate dug up one by one, while three obedient youngsters stood by and watched. The fourth scurried around to the other side of the tree and had to be brought back.

The Squirrel watched his mate shuck the cones to get at the seeds. The first few she chewed herself, to test their goodness. Then she began parceling out seeds to the babies. So! She was beginning to wean them already.

He could hardly believe it. They were indeed growing up. Now he would have to grub around for more unopened cones, while waiting for the first half-ripened seeds of the new crop. If only there were mushrooms! Perhaps in a few weeks his mate would be bold enough to lead the youngsters to the edge of the marsh for a feast of beetles and grasshoppers.

One of the bucks rose suddenly to his feet, and the unexpected movement frightened the three smaller squirrels. Their mother hurried them up the tree. The fourth youngster stood his ground, even advancing a curious step toward the deer. With an angry growl his mother whisked back and drove him up the trunk.

The Squirrel saw the buck, half-crazed by stinging flies, go swinging his head toward an open place at the edge of the woods. There he could sweep the flies from his flanks without running the risk of hitting his tender antlers, still in the velvet, against a branch or tree trunk.

The buck stamped the ground as he tried to rid himself of flies, and sent up a cloud of dust. This the Squirrel noticed with interest. A dust bath might be a good way to rid himself of some of his own parasites! He would roll in the dry, trampled dirt the first chance he had.

After a few more sweeps of his head, the buck walked into the deeper shadows of the woods past the resting deer. One by one they rose and followed him.

Now that he had the idea of a dust bath, the Squirrel was eager to leave his tree. Besides, he was parched for a drink, and like most wild folk he found thirst harder to bear than hunger. He had not had a drink since early morning when he risked a trip to the stream that emptied into the beaver pond. As fresh water close to his domain became harder to find, he became more thirsty! The persistent dry weather drove him to take chances he never had to take before.

What had happened to everything—to the ferns and senecio that used to grow along the eastern boundary of his homestead, their heads in the shade and their feet in the wet black earth? To patches of velvety moss, cool and springy under the Squirrel's paws, that used to hug the ground near the spring? To dew that used to sparkle early in the morning in big silver drops on grass and flowers?

Other summers, enough dew usually collected during the

night to give the Squirrel his first drink of the day. Now a night of dew was rare.

And other summers, a little spring kept a dark hole near the edge of the marsh full of clear water. That was one reason the Squirrel had chosen this place for his homestead in the first place. He liked water that was fresh, not stagnant. But now the spring flowed so slowly that a thick green scum had formed on top of the water, making it distasteful to him.

He stretched, lying flat on the branch and clawing as far ahead as he could reach with his forepaws, then pulling his hind legs up. He rubbed his cheeks against the bark. Then with a jerk he jumped to his feet. First he would cut across a corner of the marsh and drink at the stream; then he would roll in the loose dirt the deer had trampled.

Gracefully he slithered down the tree trunk.

His journey to the stream was made in quick leaps punctuated by cautious pauses. The air hummed with the sound of thousands of insects enjoying the heat and openness of the marsh. Never in the Squirrel's memory had he seen so many small darting wings and jumping legs.

He felt the heat, yet it seemed a good time for him to be abroad. Most of his enemies would be sleeping the afternoon away.

Near the stream he caught a fat grasshopper sunning itself on a stone, and ate it with relish. A cicado shrilled. He leaped after it, but missed. For consolation he pounced on a beetle. He had a taste for insects, and plenty lay around him, yet he disliked the sun-drenched marsh and the shimmering brightness of the nearby beaver pond. Being away from the shade and trees for even a few minutes made him fidgety.

Still, on his way back from the stream, he took time to roll in the dirt at the edge of the woods. He always tried to keep his fur, and especially his tail, well groomed by daily combing and cleaning. Every time a drop of pitch or resin stuck to his coat, he diligently bit at it or rubbed it off. But in spite of all his grooming, parasites persisted. He would shake them in the dust!

Just as he was beginning to enjoy himself, lying on his back and wriggling in the loose dirt, his fun was interrupted. A sharp cry sounded from one of his trees.

Had an enemy come in his absence?

Cautiously he flipped over and sat on his haunches, to stare at his home trees. Round ears alert, nostrils dilating, he waited. He heard quick claws scratching on bark, then silence.

Rising high on his hind feet, he thrust his head forward

for a better look. At that moment a pine marten started down the trunk of the limber pine. Had the marten caught his mate or the young ones? Had the marten seen him move?

The marten's quick eyes had caught the movement of the Squirrel wriggling in the dirt. Dashing down the tree trunk, he headed straight for the open place where the deer had stamped.

The Squirrel stared in panic. His strength seemed to flow out of him, from his legs, from his head, from his heart.

Where could he go? The marten, between him and the woods, cut off any approach to trees where his greatest safety lay. His only other choice was the marsh. Panic-stricken, his tail low, the Squirrel whirled and raced toward the beaver pond.

He could hear the marten bounding after him.

He had eluded pine martens before. By running along a branch too slender to hold the weight of a marten, and leaping to another slender branch, the Squirrel could gain time in the treetops. But on the ground he could do nothing . . . except race ahead.

In leaps of four and five feet, he jumped over dry potholes from hump to hump of marsh grass. He darted through willow brush where shoots growing close together slowed down the speed of the larger marten.

When he reached the shore of the shrunken pond, he hesitated for the fraction of a second before jumping into the water. He knew he could swim, though he rarely had occasion to. And he had a notion that martens disliked getting their feet wet.

Ahead, a mound of sticks rose out of the water. The Squirrel took refuge on it, in a shadowy crevice. Out of one eye he saw a beaver watching him from the pond.

He heard the marten snarling as it ran angrily up and down the bank. After that came the light thud of pouncing paws and the terror-squeak of a mouse. Then silence.

The beaver disappeared under the water, leaving a circle of bubbles behind her. The Squirrel waited. He was safe beneath the sticks and, with the sun under a cloud, the roof did not seem too hot. Soon late-afternoon shadows would begin to move down from the mountains. He must get home before dark somehow. . . .

Strain his ears as he might, he could hear no sound to tell him if the marten still lurked on the bank.

He could hear faint murmurings rising from beneath the roof of the beaver house. Muffled and muted in their passage through the woven sticks, the sounds reminded him of the whimpering of baby squirrels. And that reminded him of his mate in the limber pine. Had the marten found the nest?

He saw the beaver again, swimming slowly toward the lodge. Though he felt no fear of her, he knew the time had come for him to leave. With dusk approaching, the old horned owl would be getting restless for the hunt, and a squirrel would be no match for an owl in the openness of the marsh.

Darting to the top of the lodge, he satisfied himself that no enemies were prowling close to the shrunken pond. He scrambled to the edge of the roof, dove in, and swam ashore, holding his tail high and dry behind him.

The valley lay in shadow, not the cool shadow a pine squirrel had a right to expect so high above sea level, but the lazy shadow of a dry summer. The moon, nearing full, was already up, waiting until after sunset to switch on its light. Nighthawks had begun to play over the marsh. One zoomed close to the Squirrel's head in a powerful, noisy dive; but the Squirrel was not afraid. It was not like other hawks with grasping talons.

Near the edge of the woods that dipped toward the stream, the Squirrel caught a glimpse of the deer again, as they emerged from the spruces. Not another creature appeared as he made his way homeward with bounding leaps and wary pauses.

He ran immediately to the limber pine. At its base the scent of marten, still strong on the cones and shucks dug up by his mate earlier that afternoon, made him stop and sniff. The marten, running with his nose to the ground while the Squirrel was getting his drink, must have caught the scent of the squirrel family and raced up the tree to investigate.

Prepared for the worst, the Squirrel dashed up the trunk. He barked eagerly at the nest-hole, noting fresh scratches on the bark around it. The marten had tried to claw his way in by enlarging the opening, but had not succeeded.

The Squirrel's mate, with an answering chirr, popped her head out of the hole. She was safe! And he could hear sleepy whimperings that told him the young ones were safe, too.

Not until the next day did the Squirrel discover that one of the youngsters, the wilful one, the impatient one, had less than half a tail. The rest of it he had lost to the marten!

A Break in the Drought

1

BY THE END of the first week in August, the water in the pond was so low the Beaver no longer felt safe. Day after day she dredged in the mud near the burrow to keep the water deep in one place at least.

The old beaver house now stood high and dry at one end of the pond, separated from the shore by a strip of slimy mud with a large boulder in the middle. A few wilted lily pads lay in a tangle in too-shallow water, and the dam stood well above the water level of the pond. Never had the water been so low. Never in the Beaver's memory had such a long dry spell afflicted the mountain valley.

Squatting in the cramped quarters of the stuffy burrow, with her youngsters sleeping around her, she combed her fur automatically. What could she do? Even though she felt unsafe in the shrunken pond, leaving it would be more dangerous than staying. And where could she go? If she left with the family, how would her mate be able to find them when he returned?

With the water so low, getting food had become a real problem. The danger in reaching willow brush and aspens increased as the pond shrank. Safety lay in keeping close to water, not in waddling around on shore where the fastest beaver moved more slowly than the slowest enemy.

The last canal had dried under the thirsty sun. Now only mud-cracked channels led into the willow brush. Grass and flowers, juicy and plentiful two months before, had become dry and unappetizing.

The Beaver faced uncertainty and danger in the shallow pond. With good grace she carried the responsibility for the feeding, comfort, and security of her two kits and four yearlings. Yet the summer continued to work against her.

So far she and the young ones had been able to find food without encountering enemies. But as each day passed and the risk increased, the strain of responsibility began to tell on her. She looked thin and worn.

She turned to settle down in her bed for an early afternoon sleep, then changed her mind. First, she would slip out into the pond to see if there was any chance of rain. Every afternoon she did this. But except for a few scattered showers, that cooled the air temporarily and the water in the pond not at all, no rain had fallen.

Emerging from the short tunnel, she startled a number of fish resting in the shadow of the tunnel entrance. They darted this way and that before vanishing under the bank. Fish had become a problem; there were too many of them now in too small a space. As the water level fell, they had crowded into the deep end of the pond near the burrow.

A number of them had been trapped in pockets of water as the pond shrank around them. There they became easy prey for bobcats and coyotes, and even for a lumbering black bear who visited the pond one night. Several nights the beaver dared not go ashore for food because of enemies that came to catch the trapped fish.

Now the pockets were empty, the fish were gone.

The Beaver surfaced for a look at the weather. The sky had clouded over. Except for a small patch of sunlight on the marsh, the valley lay in shadow. The air was oppressively heavy. In other summers this would have meant a storm was on the way, but this year nothing happened as it should!

She watched the last patch of sunlight blink out. Lowering clouds pressed shadows over the marsh and a stir of cooler air suddenly riffled across the water. A crash of thunder echoed among the peaks at the head of the valley.

This had happened nearly every afternoon for weeks, yet little rain had fallen. Today, though, the air had a different smell. The Beaver, treading water, sniffed and waited.

Another thunderclap, frightening in its intensity, rumbled down the valley. Birds flew over the marsh, seeking protection in the aspens and the dark trees to the north. For a few minutes the sky held its breath, then trembled and roared again. Another blinding flash came, and a loud crack. The Beaver ducked her head. That was close! Lightning had struck a tree near the edge of the marsh.

In a few minutes she surfaced again, expecting to smell the coming of rain, the wonderful damp coolness of breaking rain clouds. Yet not a drop fell.

She sniffed again. The frightening smell of smoke came drifting over the marsh, faint to be sure, yet strong enough to stir memories of smoke that had hung over the pond for days two years ago. At that time her mate was back from his summer journey; the pond was full and cool, the beaver house surrounded by water. This time she was alone with the kits and yearlings in a pond so shallow it would be sorry protection against fire spreading across the marsh.

She hurried back to the burrow. At least, her family would be safer in the den than in the lodge with its walls of dry sticks and mud. She would have to keep watch; if the fire spread toward the pond. . . .

Something hit the earth roof with a thud. Then came another muffled thud, then another. She sat on her haunches, her short round ears alert. This could not be rain! Rain never pounded that hard. Only a foot of earth between den and sky kept the roof from collapsing under the beating.

The kits whimpered and crowded against her.

Finally she could stand the suspense no longer. With murmured warnings to the youngsters to stay quiet, she slipped into the pond.

A strange sight met her eyes. The pond was roofed over with a layer of bobbing ice balls. Great hailstones continued to thunder down, bouncing and splashing above her. Her ears hummed with the roar of the pelting, her heart beat with the excitement of the wild storm. Fascinated, she swam under the swaying ice. Already she could feel a stir of freshness, a slight cooling in the water.

Hail was still thundering down when she had to return to the den to breathe. Where a little air came in around the roots of an old stump drops of melted ice were filtering through. She churred at her frightened youngsters to assure them all was well.

Later the hail turned to rain, a hard pounding rain, then to a sun-bright drizzle. In an hour it was all over. But what an hour!

The Beaver poked her head through the thick layer of hailstones on the pond. They parted before her. A refreshing coldness touched her head and slid from her fur. She rose and dove, rose and dove again through the hailstones.

She brought her youngsters to sport beside her. Sliding under one of the solemn-faced kits, she lifted him on her back and swam through the exhilarating coldness.

The marsh glittered under its blanket of hailstones. The stream, swollen beyond its banks, roared along with a burden of ice, water, silt, and debris, pouring its burden into the beaver pond. Quickly shallow places disappeared; water rose against the dam. The boulder in the channel between the beaver house and shore became smaller and smaller, until it was hidden altogether. Potholes in the marsh began to fill and beaver canals began to look like canals again.

Joyfully the Beaver swam around the deepening pond. The air had the frosty freshness of a winter morning. Cold hailstones on sun-baked earth and warm pond water sent up a steam of mist that filtered the sunlight and turned the mountain world into an unreal place.

She could not get enough of sniffing the moistness. She forgot about the smell of smoke before the storm. Not a trace of it remained.

On the ruined slopes at the head of the valley, the storm had struck with the same fury. Hail pounded the slopes, loosening what litter remained around stumps and rocks, and tore into the exposed soil. Later the pelting rain washed away hail and litter and earth, rushing its plunder to the stream that emptied into the beaver pond.

In some places on the slopes, where stately Engelmann spruces had grown only two years before, bare rock showed after the storm.

Once the forest there had helped to create soil. Tree roots, forcing their way into cracks in rocks, broke them to pieces. Rain worked on them and broke them still further. Fallen needles and twigs and bark added humus. Slowly over the centuries soil had been building up . . . only to be swept away in one pounding storm.

The Beaver watched the yearlings, mad with delight, playing tag through the floating hailstones. Big-eyed, the kits followed her as she swam underwater to investigate all the changes in the pond. Enough water already filled the channel so they could circle the beaver house, and water still poured in.

For several hours after the storm, water kept rushing down the valley. Up, up crept the water along the dam, until it reached the top and swirled over. The Beaver's world had changed quickly from dryness and despair to fullness and joy. Now even though the pond would shrink again if the drought returned, enough water would remain to assure safety and comfort until her mate came home in early September.

At the dam a surprise awaited her. Accumulated debris, washed-down branches and sticks, made the dam appear double its usual thickness. Slowly she swam the length of the barrier that backed the water into a temporary lake. A few more storms like this and the pond would fill with silt and trash.

The hail melted on the pond faster than it melted on land and the water became as cold and invigorating as in late fall. The Beaver led the way into the marsh. Now willows and aspens lay within safe reach. But something had happened to the willow brush! When she reached for a twig, she found it almost stripped of leaves. On the muddy ground beneath the shrubs, and floating on the dark water, lay a scum of leaves torn off by the hail. The long-awaited storm had brought destruction as well as bounty.

Like the willows, the aspens were stripped of most of

their greenery. A mat of shredded leaves covered the ground in the grove, and the beavers had a feast without having to work for it.

Grass and flower stalks lay beaten into the mud. Much of the summer food of the Beaver and her family was gone, its life pounded out by the hail. Yet safety had returned to the pond. This must be a night of play, a night of celebration!

The Beaver swung toward the old lodge to await the full coming of night. Her youngsters followed, excited by all the unexpected changes. They sculled up the tunnel into the old familiar room, only to find it no longer familiar. Clumps of mud, cracked and loosened by the drought and dislodged by the hail and rain, lay spattered over the floor. Here and there through unplastered sticks of the roof came glints of the gray sky of dusk.

They went outside to examine the dome of the lodge. So much mud had been washed away, it looked more like a pile of debris than a beaver house. Scrambling over the rough sticks, the Beaver saw that a great deal of work would have to be done to make the house tight again for winter. But the structure was still firm.

They dove back into the pond again, full of eagerness and play.

Whack! The unexpected sound of a beaver tail slapping the water followed by the hollow plunging sound of a dive, broke the darkening silence around the pond.

The beavers were under water in a flash. Someone had come into their pond.

Cautiously the mother Beaver surfaced. A dark form was swimming toward her. Could it be her mate, returning ahead of time? Had he come back because of the drought, because of dangerously low water in the streams? She waited, peering into the dusk, twitching her nose.

Before the strange beaver reached her, she knew it was not her mate. A friendly visitor had stopped at the pond, an old fellow with gray whiskers. Scars on his grizzled face and a torn ear showed him to be a veteran fighter.

Almost at once he began to sport with the yearlings, as if he missed his own family left behind in some other valley. They raced and chased all over the pond; they climbed on the dam to wrestle. But the four yearlings together were no match for the experienced oldster.

Strange beavers had visited the pond before, in other summers, but the Beaver hardly expected one to venture up so dry a valley this summer. One day earlier the stranger would have found the pond a sorry place. Now he could join in their night of fun and feasting.

They splashed and chased and nibbled at aspen and willow leaves and twigs, and splashed and chased again under a sky washed clean of the dust and heat of summer. They played all the games they knew and invented others. Never had stars sparkled more brightly, never had the crescent of a moon given more light.

And then came an unexpected end to the fun.

The Beavers were all on shore, eating from broken aspen branches, nipping and chewing the few leaves left on the twigs. Suddenly the mother Beaver raised her head to listen and sniff. Had she caught a whiff of enemy scent? Rising on her haunches, she turned her head from side to side to sniff. Only a gentle breeze, hardly a breeze at all, blew off the pond. It brought the moist smell of coolness and cleanness, nothing more.

Caution had become so ingrained in her during the trying summer that she decided to play safe by taking the kits to the burrow. They had eaten their fill, anyway; they had played themselves tired. She churred to the kits to follow her.

Before they were halfway across the pond, she heard frightening sounds from the aspen grove. A sharp beaver hiss! A snarl and snapping of teeth! Sending the kits on to the burrow, she turned back, full of concern for the yearlings. Why were they not rushing for safety in the pond?

She heard a whacking splash in the pond.

As she pulled herself to the muddy bank, another yearling plunged past her. In the dark the smell of fresh blood reached her. Where were the other yearlings?

Noise of a scramble ahead told of a fight in progress. Anxiously she called. A third yearling, limping badly, humped toward her, then scuttled on to the pond. Had the ailing one, the slower one, been unable to escape in time?

Before she reached the fighters, her nose told her that the enemy was a bobcat. She hesitated, then pushed on, almost stumbling over the missing yearling lying on the ground beside a log, injured and bleeding, but still alive.

The visiting beaver was fighting for his life after going to the rescue of the yearlings. But although he was a good ten pounds heavier than the bobcat, he was no match for its agility and cunning. His teeth and claws were made for peaceful work, not for fighting. His low-slung body moved slowly and clumsily compared to the lithe enemy.

Without hesitation the Beaver plunged into the fight. She gave a menacing hiss and snapped at the bobcat's throat.

Missing her mark, she caught hold of an ear with her sharp front teeth. The bobcat yowled and turned toward her long enough for the other beaver to get a grip on one of the cat's front paws. Then the grizzled fellow began to pull his captive in the direction of the pond.

The Beaver kept snapping angrily at the bobcat's throat after losing her hold on his ear. All the while the other beaver kept tugging. He was trying to pull the clawing, biting enemy into the pond! Water was the beaver's element, not the bobcat's. If the cat could be held under water. . . .

She felt a sting of pain as the bobcat's teeth made a gash between her eyes. Biting back, she caught the torn ear again.

They were moving closer, closer to the pond, both beavers getting punishing bites from the enemy. But the grizzled one refused to loosen his hold on the bobcat's paw.

At last they were on the bank, teetering as they clawed and hissed and snapped at each other. With a desperate burst of energy the old beaver succeeded in toppling the bobcat into the water and dragging it under.

For a short time the bobcat thrashed around in the pond. Then it sank, still fighting, pulled down to the depths by the strong and tenacious beaver.

Oblivious of her gashes and cuts, the Beaver hurried back to the grove to the injured yearling. He was whimpering with pain. Sniffing him, nuzzling him, she tried to help him to his feet, but each time he slumped and fell back again. She dared not leave him alone in the grove.

After several attempts at lifting him, she succeeded in clasping him to her breast with her forepaws, as she had often carried stones for the dam. He was a more awkward burden, but she managed to rise on her hind feet and waddle to the pond with him.

Somehow she swam across the pond and up the tunnel to the burrow. There she could care for him in safety. After settling him in his bed and comforting him, she swam back to find the old beaver who had fought so bravely to save the yearlings.

She found him trying to tug the bobcat's body through the debris packed in front of the dam by the storm. With great effort he finally pulled the bobcat over the dam into the stream below. Old warrior that he was, he wanted to clear the pond of all signs of the enemy.

As the Beaver swam near, he settled down on the dam and began to investigate his wounds. He was bleeding from several deep gashes and there was an ugly tear in the fur on his neck. Yet there he sat mumbling cheerfully, as if a good fight was all part of a night's work.

2

Ground squirrels and chipmunks lay deep in their dens sleeping away the heat of August, while the Pine Squirrel brooded in his favorite tree. Summer had turned out to be his most persistent enemy, more unnerving than the occasional four-footed enemy that invaded his domain.

It was not the Squirrel's habit to avoid disagreeable weather by sleeping for long periods of time, winter or summer. His distant cousin the ground squirrel slept almost two-thirds of its life away. That little nuisance the chipmunk, stealer of cones, slept all winter and during the hottest weeks of summer. But the Pine Squirrel met weather as it came, day after day.

True, during a long rainstorm, or windstorm, or blizzard, he might stay in his nest a few days at a time, curled up in a doze. But in summer, even so hot and dry a summer as this, he was abroad every day soon after sunrise.

On this bright August morning before the hailstorm he had been up and doing even earlier than usual. He was upset . . . and not just about weather, not just about the enervating sunlight that worked its way through the branches of his trees and patched the ground with shadows. Now he had an even greater concern: Food.

At a season of the year when food should be plentiful, when treetops should be full of cones with half-ripe seeds, getting a good meal was becoming a problem. Mushrooms refused to grow. Buds had long since blossomed into flowers that dried before their seeds were properly formed. Blueberries shriveled instead of ripening into sweet dark fruit. Even the juniper berries were falling early.

The week before, after patient searching and sniffing, the Squirrel had dug up the last cache of cones he could find. Half the seeds had been stolen by mice and chipmunks; most of the others were mouldy or sprouting.

True, grasshoppers and beetles could be had for the catching in the burnished marsh. They reveled in the heat and persistent dryness. Yet the Squirrel's appetite for insects was limited, and going to catch them involved a certain amount of danger. Coyotes came to the marsh to feast on insects, especially grasshoppers; martens and weasels came to dart among the willow clumps; squirrel-catching hawks swooped unexpectedly out of the cloudless sky.

The Squirrel's gravest concern was the drought-blighted condition of the cone crop in his part of the forest.

For a long time he had sensed that all was not well in the treetops. At first, summer had followed its usual pattern.

Clouds of pollen blew through the woods in June like sun-flecked dust. After blossoms fell from the tops of the firs and spruces, little cones began to form, in the usual way. But dry weather and hot sun kept them from developing.

In the high forest where the Squirrel lived, cones normally clustered near the light, at the tops of trees. Small, light-colored cones of Engelmann spruces hung down, pointing toward the ground. Larger purple-black cones of alpine firs stood upright on the twigs, pointing toward the sky. But where were the clusters this year? Where were the cones to harvest?

Early that morning the Squirrel had again gone carefully over every tree in his homestead. Here and there a few cones had managed to grow. He did not, of course, expect them to be ripe in early August when his harvest usually began. His instinct told him that he must always cut them green and store them away to mature before their scales opened and the seeds escaped.

Nearly every cone he examined was malformed or stunted, and the seeds were small and shrunken. Where was he to find the almost three hundred cones he would need for his winter supply? Harvest time was at hand and there was nothing to harvest.

If it came to the worst, he would keep from starving by eating the inner bark of twigs. It was tender and edible enough, and certainly the supply was limitless. But bark was a poor substitute for seeds and nuts. He could not face a winter without cones.

After searching his own trees that morning, he had swung through the woods to see how other trees fared. He went north past the blue jay's tree that stood like a sentinel above others, the old lightning gash a long scar down its trunk.

Circling, he came out at a point south of his range close to the beaver pond.

His findings disturbed him. Not many cones grew in tree-tops within harvesting distance of home. And he had seen several other squirrels busy cutting the few cones there were.

As he sat on a limb, hot and dispirited, he saw his mate come out to give the young ones their daily lesson.

They were two and a half months old now, almost half-grown. Agile and well disciplined, they had learned their lessons well—except for the wilful one.

For a week after losing his tail he had sulked in the nest. When he finally joined the others in their lessons, he found that most of the things he had learned involved using his tail in one way or another—as a rudder, a balancing pole, a parachute. Without a tail, he felt insecure and unsure of himself. Instead of leading, he had to follow.

Today the Squirrel's mate was drilling the young ones in running along a branch and jumping to a slightly lower limb on the next tree. It was an easy jump. The first three young-sters made it easily, automatically using their tails for bal-ance. But the tailless one, in an effort to make a longer and more impressive leap than the others, came to grief.

Landing too near the curving edge of the branch, two of his feet found nothing to cling to. The inside hind foot slipped, putting all the youngster's weight on one gripping forepaw. For a second or two he dangled there, trying des-perately to pull himself back to the branch. But before he could dig the claws of his other forepaw into the bark, he lost his grip.

Down, down he fell! Without a spread-out tail to break the force of his fall, he plummeted to the ground, striking the sharp edge of a boulder as he passed. He lay quiet, half-hidden in a patch of juniper.

With a sharp cry the Squirrel's mate raced down the tree. He followed. Leaping recklessly, they jumped into the prickly juniper to sniff and tug at the limp body lying there. They chirred and chattered. But the youngster did not stir.

The Squirrel could see that his mate yearned to carry her baby to the safety of the nest, but he was too heavy to lift as a dead weight. If he could curl around his mother's throat, in the squirrel way, with legs and tail around her neck, she could get a grip on the scruff of his belly and carry him. But he lay quiet in the juniper.

The Squirrel gave up first. These things happened . . . he accepted them as part of life. Silently he went back to his lookout. For a while his mate hovered over the youngster; then she, too, abandoned him. He would scamper through the treetops no more.

Suddenly the Squirrel felt the need for action. For too many days he had been moping. In his circuit through the woods that morning activity had taken his mind off his troubles. He would go farther this time, westward toward timber line, to see if he could find any cones!

He jerked to attention and, whisking to the end of the limb, leaped to the next tree. Then he was off on the high dark road of branches.

No matter where he looked, he found no hope for a harvest. A few cones here, a few there, a cluster or two beyond, gave him scant encouragement. They were too few and far away to harvest.

Nearing the head of the valley, he came upon the burned-over slopes with scattered charred trunks still standing and bare rock showing where the soil had been washed away.

Nothing but desolation here—not a cone on all those acres that once supported a thriving forest! He stopped in a tree-top at the edge of the burning, wondering what to do next.

Past the charred derelicts rose rocky heights and tundra-covered slopes patched with greenery of dwarfed timber-line trees. Dare he venture across the burned slopes to investigate the far clumps of green? He decided against it. The danger of open spaces was ingrained in him, and he had already seen enough to know that something had blighted the entire cone crop.

As he looked, clouds eclipsed the last patch of sunlight on the burned-over slopes. A roll of thunder rumbled among the peaks. His whiskers twitched nervously.

A flock of pine grosbeaks with strong, stubby beaks came

twitting into the tree where he sat. He watched them quietly. They, too, were scouting through the woods in quest of food. Whistling cheerily at one another, occasionally bursting into song, they seemed not to be depressed by the absence of cones. But then they covered great distances with little effort, and in a few weeks would be moving down to lower altitudes. The Squirrel, living in the mountains winter and summer, had to find enough cones here to tide him over months of cold weather.

In a moment the grosbeaks rose in a body and swept to another tree, busily discussing what to do next and where to go.

Two nutcrackers flew over, cawing loudly. They depended on cone seeds even more than the grosbeaks, and liked to winter in the mountains. The Squirrel was not the only one with a food problem.

Clouds were beginning to press lower on the mountains and a swell of cool air suddenly swept down from the heights. Another roll of thunder filled the valley with foreboding. The Squirrel sniffed. Was this to be more than a storm threat that died away before enough rain fell to do any good? All summer long, rain seemed to tremble on the brink of afternoon clouds without finding the strength to spill over.

This time a really loud crash of thunder echoed down the valley. The Squirrel whirled and galloped homeward.

He did not like thunderstorms—the noise frightened him, the piercing flashes of lightning blinded him. Even in the snugness of his nest, with its roof and door-flap to keep out rain, he trembled. Certainly he did not want to be caught in a storm away from home in strange trees. Forgetting all about cones and harvests, he raced along.

A bright flash of light ripped across the woods in front of him. Almost immediately on the heavy air came the sharp crack of a tree struck by the bolt. It seemed to come from the direction of his domain! He rushed ahead.

In the dim past the Squirrel remembered being shaken and almost toppled from the family nest when the nest-tree was split by lightning. Rain had poured in on him and his brothers and sisters, in spite of their mother hovering over them.

As he neared home, a sharp smell struck his nostrils and brought him to an abrupt stop. He sniffed carefully. Smoke! A pall of the same smell had hung over the valley for more than a week during the forest fire two years before. This was only a wisp by comparison, but it made him tremble.

He dashed on.

The woods had grown as dark as dusk with clouds pressing down. Everything seemed to be holding its breath— birds, trees, the heavy air. Ahead lay his cherished homestead, and ahead lay the source of the smoke. Was the nest safe?

He found his mate running excitedly back and forth, calling him. The smell of smoke frightened her, too. With relief the Squirrel saw that his trees were safe; the smoke came from farther north. They whisked to the top of a spruce to look. . . .

The blue jays' tree was on fire! Black smoke swirled up and eager flames crackled in the same pitchy gash where lightning had struck years before. So far only the long scar was ablaze, but if the fire spread. . . .

Another crash of thunder, another blinding streak of lightning battered the woods as the squirrels watched. A slight wind sprang up, just enough to fan the flames and make them leap higher as they ate at the fatty pitch.

The Squirrel must be ready to lead his family away at a moment's notice if the fire should sweep to other trees, but he did not know where to lead them. He remembered the beaver house where he had taken refuge from the marten weeks before, not knowing that it now loomed high and dry above the shrunken pond.

Suddenly, with a thud, something struck the branch on which the squirrels were sitting. Something hit a twig and set it swaying. Thud. Thud. Balls of frosty ice began crashing through the branches. This was no time to sit and watch a fire! The squirrels raced for cover.

Just as the hailstorm broke in thundering fury, the Squirrel reached his nest. Stones of ice struck branches around him and pounded on the roof of the forest. His nest in a crotch of the tree was protected by trunks on both sides and by branches above, yet bouncing hailstones found their way through to crash on his roof.

He curled into himself, his ears full of the relentless pounding roar. It seemed as if all the clouds that had hung above the forest during the summer had opened to pour out their icy burden.

Never in the Squirrel's memory had there been such a hailstorm. Almost at once the air seeping into his nest turned cool, then cold, like the breath of winter itself. His roof began to leak. For the first time all summer he was aware of the thinness of his coat. And still the hail came pounding down, tearing twigs and branches and needles from the trees.

After a while the hail turned to rain that pelted furiously on trees and ground. The Squirrel crouched in the driest corner of his nest, trembling with cold and fear.

Not until the storm was over, except for the drip, drip, drip from the branches, did he venture to poke his nose out the door. Below, the ground was covered with hailstones. Needles and boughs torn from the trees lay scattered around. The branches of his nest-tree were bedecked with hard white stones caught in pockets and furrows between needles.

Shivering, yet spurred on by curiosity, he hurried to the top of a tree for a look at the strange world. Cold drops which he shook on himself in passing made him wetter and more shivery than ever. When he looked toward the blue jays' tree he could see a few wisps of steam still coming from its deep wound. The smoke and flames had vanished.

As returning sunlight glinted into the woods, the icy floor began to send steamy mist into the trees. The Squirrel had to move about to keep warm.

Chattering with cold and excitement, he scurried to the limber pine tree. His mate was poking her head out of the nest-hole, sniffing the air. He urged her to come out and chase with him through the wet treetops. To his surprise she came, frisking toward him. Flip and away they went, wild and carefree again, as if they had suddenly been whisked back to the middle of April.

Dangerous Journey

1

AFTER THE HAILSTORM the drought returned; a dry sun came back to shine on the mountain valley. For the fourth month rainfall was well below normal.

By early September the beaver pond had shrunk again, though it was not so low as before the hailstorm. The lake that had spread over the marsh vanished, and only one canal still contained enough water for swimming. Again the Beaver was beginning to be concerned for her family's safety in the dwindling pond.

She had only three yearlings to watch over now instead of four, and one of them still limped. The undersized one, mangled by the bobcat, had lived only a few days. She had hovered over him, licking him and bringing him food. But he was too feeble to recover from his injuries.

She missed him as she had never missed a young one before. Ever since the spring famine he, more than any of the others, had depended on her.

Yet the memory of her loss soon faded. In her life only the present mattered, the present and its relation to the future. The past vanished like morning mist over the beaver pond.

The beavers slept through the most of the heat of the day

in the poorly ventilated darkness of the burrow. They usually ate at dawn and again in early evening now that the grass was dry and they were back on their diet of aspen twigs. Freshly peeled sticks floated near shore or were caught in the rubbish behind the dam. By night the beavers took their exercise and fun.

One night, about two weeks after the fight with the bobcat, the Beaver was cutting a medium-sized aspen in the grove. She had left her kits in the den, and kept warning the yearlings to stay out of the way. She never could be sure how a tree would fall.

At the ominous cracking sound that told when a tree was about to crash, the yearlings scurried off, the Beaver turned and ran. But the youngster with the sore foot did not scamper fast enough. As the tree fell its upper branches grazed him and knocked him off his feet. He squealed more from fright than from pain, but the accident might have cost him his life.

Gradually the water in the pond had become warm again. Other years, the mountain stream and underground spring together kept the water pleasantly cool even under a bright sun. Now the stream flowed languidly again; the spring, after bubbling up for a week or two following the hailstorm, had died down to almost nothing.

Runoff from the storm on the burned-over slopes had been too fast for moisture to work its way underground. Only trickles from the last melting snowbanks on the heights found their way to the stream.

The old beaver had stayed at the pond for a few days after the fight, waiting for his wounds to heal. He rested and sunned himself and slept; he nibbled at aspen bark and rested again. Instead of sporting with the yearlings, he conserved his strength. And then one night he had quietly vanished.

The Beaver was not surprised to find him gone. With the busy season only a few weeks off, the time had come for him to make his way back to his home pond. Soon he would be repairing his lodge, plastering it with a thick layer of mud. Soon he would be reinforcing his dam and cutting aspen for the winter food supply.

September was bringing coolness, especially at night, but the dry weather continued.

Near midnight on the third day of the month the Beaver and her youngsters were enjoying a game of follow-the-leader in the pond. She was leading them toward the dam, diving up and down like a porpoise. At the dam she waddled over the tangled drift of rubbish and pulled herself to the dry stick-and-mud barrier above water level. Three yearlings and two kits followed her, one after the other.

She was about to dive back into the pond, when she heard

a familiar throaty noise on the other side of the dam. Instantly she stood on her hind feet, listening and sniffing. In turn, the five youngsters followed suit.

"Chrrrr," came the sound again.

The Beaver answered. The young ones answered.

She hurried eagerly along the dam to meet the dark figure scrambling up from below. Her mate had returned! They touched noses and nibbled each other's cheeks in delight.

The yearlings and kits pressed close to share in the reunion. Soon the entire family was sporting in the pond. The limping yearling, not handicapped in the water by his injury, swam as fast and tirelessly as the others. They were together again—one less than before, but all in good spirits despite the unusual hardships of the summer.

Eager to show her mate the changes in the pond, the Beaver began to lead him around . . . to the mud-caked canals, the shallow mountain stream, the dead spring, the new deposits of silt and rubbish, the lodge looming well above its normal September water level. Looking at everything, they swam around the pond with the young ones trailing in their wake.

The Beaver, sensing that something more lasting than a summer of drought was wrong with the valley, feared the coming of winter. What would keep the food pile from freezing again? What would keep the pond from freezing to the very tunnel of the lodge itself?

The next night the weather turned cold and windy. Watching her mate, the Beaver waited for a lead. If he intended to stay at the pond, it seemed like a good time to start repairing the lodge. She and the yearlings would help plaster the house when he made the first move to dig mud from the pond bottom.

But her mate showed little interest in work. Slowly and carefully he swam around, looking at everything again. He followed one of the muddy canals into the drying marsh. He ventured upstream a way. When he returned, he cut an aspen sapling and called his family to eat and idle the night away.

The next night, as if still reluctant to come to a decision, he spent hours upstream. The Beaver understood his reluctance. Home was a precious place to her, too, a hard place to abandon. In this pond she had been born; in this pond she had raised five families of kits. Yet if it was time to leave, she must not hesitate to strike out for a new home.

The third night she saw her mate idling again. Time was slipping away. Winter came early in the mountains, and the family must not be caught unprepared. Something told the Beaver it would be folly to repair the lodge and gather a food pile in the dwindling pond. They must leave the valley or perish.

Resolutely she swam to one end of the dam. She called. The kits came and the yearlings, but not her mate. Standing on the dam, looking back through the starlit darkness, she churred once more. Then she scrambled down to the small stream fed by seepage through the dam.

Before her down the valley lay unknown country, made more mysterious by enfolding night. Behind her lay the pond she would never see again. Mumbling encouragement to her youngsters, she moved ahead.

She had not gone far before her mate came barging after her, nudging the young ones out of the way, pressing to get ahead. With the decision made at last, he could not move fast enough! She stepped aside and waited for the young ones to file ahead of her. For safety's sake she would bring up the rear.

Her mate chose to continue along the stream, although the water was too low to offer any protection. Still, enough flowed down the valley to wash over their tracks, erasing the scent from an enemy.

The going was hard. In places the course was strewn with rocks and debris; then again it oozed with mud. Webbed feet were made for pushing a beaver through yielding water, not for walking along a rough stream bed. The youngsters whimpered. The yearling was limping badly.

The wind, blowing as usual from the mountains, came from behind them. The Beaver would have preferred to face into it, so they would have advance notice of enemies ahead. With the wind at their backs, their own scent blew ahead of them, bringing news of their coming to any enemy lurking downstream.

They plodded on. A waning moon, just rising in the east, was beginning to probe the valley with long slim fingers of light. This made the open strip of stream bed easier for the beavers to see, yet at the same time exposed them to enemy eyes.

Everything was frightening and strange. Even such familiar sounds as wind in treetops and water trickling over rocks made the beavers nervous.

From the woods came the alarming "hoo, hoo-hoo, hoo, hoo" of an owl hoping to scare a mouse or rabbit into motion. The quavering call of a coyote rang between distant hills.

Under the roots of an upturned pine the beavers sought the shelter of deep shadows while they rested. The Beaver knew from the smell that a marten had been there not long before. Between old roots he had dug out a family of mice. Their nest, a ball of soft shredded grass, lay torn and empty.

While the beavers huddled together resting, another hoot came, too close for comfort. Then they heard the thump of paws running along the bank as a snowshoe rabbit sped by. For a fraction of a second the Beaver caught a glint of light on mottled wings sweeping past—the silent, ghostly wings of an owl.

Suddenly, ahead of them, they heard the terrified squeal of a rabbit.

The beavers waited, listening and sniffing, until impatience forced them on again. As they passed a low place in the bank, they found a tuft of rabbit fur and an owl feather.

The mother Beaver crowded close to her kits. She must not let them fall behind for an instant, with an owl patrolling the valley. She must be more cautious than ever. If only the stream carried enough water for swimming, how much simpler their journey would be.

The kits began to whimper as they stumbled ahead. In their three short months of life they had only waddled along the grassy bank of the beaver pond. Now they had to scramble over and around rocks and through reefs of debris left by the hailstorm. Their little legs rebelled. The limping yearling complained, too, as he hobbled along.

Where was her mate leading them? The Beaver had no idea how far they were going or how long it would take. She knew only that the possibility of survival lay ahead; certain starvation lay behind.

The important thing was to stay together, to keep the young ones from lagging. Her mate must be aware of this too, yet he drove ahead, impatient to lead his family to safety. She had to urge him to slow down and to help boost the kits over logs and boulders and through rough places. By helping the kits, they would make better time in the end.

The injured yearling had to manage as best he could.

They came to a place where another stream flowed into the valley from an angle in the hills. But still the water was not deep enough for swimming, except in occasional rock-lined pools. Whenever they reached a deep pool, the beavers rested in the safety of the water and gained courage to press onward. Even in the country of the unknown, water was their friend.

At a bend in the stream, where the bed was studded with boulders rising high above the shallow water, the Beaver was startled by a fresh scent. She saw her mate stand on his haunches to sniff. Here, not long before, a bobcat had jumped from stone to stone to cross to the other side. Where was he now—lurking along the shore, waiting for a chance to seize one of the young ones? She murmured to the kits to keep close to her, confident that a bobcat would not attack as long as the seven beavers stayed together.

Scent or no scent, there was nothing to do but move ahead.

She trusted her mate. He would take them to a place where there would be enough running water to build a dam that would make a pond. He might continue down the valley or double back up another stream. In any event, she expected him to follow a water course. And so she was surprised to see him hesitate at the next bend, then waddle to the bank.

For some minutes he stood there on his hind legs, his nose in the air, turning his head this way and that as if to get his bearings. Suddenly, grunting for his family to follow, he headed for the woods.

What did it mean? Did he know a short cut? The Beaver was afraid to leave the stream. Even a little water was enough to cover their footprints, and the occasional deep pools gave them needed rest and safety. On land their scent would speak loudly to any enemy who crossed their trail. They would be at the mercy of sharp teeth and tearing claws. Yet she must follow where her mate led; they must stay together.

She urged the young ones up the bank and into the woods.

Now that the moon was climbing higher, streaks of gray light cut the shadows under the evergreens and scattered aspens. For a while the beavers made better time than they had along the stream. Fewer boulders lay in their path and there were fewer logs against which brush had been piled

by the storm. But when a ridge loomed ahead, the problem of getting the young ones over the rough ground and through tangles of brush seemed unsurmountable.

Slowly they pushed ahead on their strange adventure, at the mercy of their enemies.

Before they reached the top of the ridge, they heard the triumphant cry of coyotes in the valley below. Had they picked up the beavers' scent?

Spurred on by fear, the Beaver and her mate urged the young ones to hurry across the uneven ground. Their tails were bruised from being dragged over stones and through brush. Their feet were sore, their legs weary, their strength waning. Yet there could be no prolonged resting or turning back.

Finally they reached a welcome stretch of dry grass near the top of the ridge, open to the moonlight. Before crossing they stopped to look and listen. Coyotes were still yapping in the valley. Ahead the way looked clear and safe. The beavers began to scamper across the opening.

Suddenly the Beaver stopped, rearing to her hind legs to sniff. She had caught a new scent on an eddy of wind. What now?

Another breeze brought reassurance. The Beaver hurried ahead, murmuring encouragement to her young ones. Mule deer, grazing and browsing on the ridge, had passed the grassy opening not long before. Now the beavers could rest and gather strength before continuing their journey. They could stay close to the deer and lose their scent in the deer scent.

In the shadow of a log where a deer had recently lain to chew his cud, they huddled together.

As her kits lay panting, the mother Beaver nuzzled them.

She had no way of explaining why the gruelling journey had been undertaken, no way of telling them when it would end. All she could do was to urge them to persevere.

She heard the welcome sound of deer moving through the woods, and saw two young ones cross the opening. Leaning against the log, she relaxed for the first time since they left the last deep pool.

The beavers' rest was interrupted by the renewed yapping of coyotes, coming closer and closer. They must have found the trail up the ridge! Huddling together behind the log, paralyzed with fright, the beavers waited.

An antlered buck stepped into the moonlit opening and stood, head up, listening. Closer came the eager cry of the coyotes. It sounded like a pack, yet the Beaver knew from experience it was probably only a pair. Still, seven beavers of assorted ages were no match for a pair of hungry coyotes.

Suddenly the buck wheeled and began to jump—brump! brump!—along the ridge. Other deer broke from the woods and joined him. Two yapping shapes came racing over the top of the ridge. Forgetting about the beavers in the excitement of a chase, the coyotes dashed after the deer.

Losing no time, now that the immediate danger had passed, the beavers scurried across the grassy opening to the woods on the other side of the ridge and plunged into the shadows. There, mingled with the fragrance of spruce, the faint smell of something else urged them on. Water! Somewhere ahead lay water, somewhere in the valley below the ridge. Before too long, if all went well, they would be safe! The Beaver's mate had taken them by the shortest route. . . .

Then for the first time she saw that the limping yearling was missing. She stopped and churred. The yearling, favoring his injured foot, must have lagged behind when they crossed the ridge. Impatiently she waited for a sound of him.

Ahead she could hear her mate and the others going down the wooded slope toward the water. She was torn by the desire to hurry after them and to go back to look for the yearling.

As she hesitated, she heard a hiss from the ridge, a scuffle . . . then silence. She sniffed. Was that the scent of a bobcat? She could not be sure. It would be like a bobcat to follow the trail stealthily from the stream bed and wait for a chance to pounce on a straggler.

To go back would be to expose herself to danger. Life lay ahead, not behind. Safety lay ahead in the water somewhere beyond the trees. Quickly she turned and hurried to catch up with the others blundering down the slope to a strange pond in a strange valley.

2

Dusk began to overtake the Pine Squirrel along the stream bed below the beaver pond. He was on his way back from searching for a new homesite that day in early September, and was trying to reach home before dark. But lengthening shadows stretching down the narrow valley caused him to change his mind. For several hours the sun had been blotted out by the barrier of mountains ahead.

Three days away from home had made the Squirrel yearn for the comfort and safety of his nest and a good night's sleep. He chafed with impatience to let his mate know that he had found a place to spend the winter. Yet he held himself in check and looked around for a safe place to sleep.

At dusk the horned owl would start his night of hunting. At dusk the marten and bobcat would begin tracking down scents in earnest. Now was no time for a squirrel to be taking chances. Without him, his family would face starvation. With him to lead the way, they could enjoy a plentiful supply of cones in the valley he had found where the hailstorm had not struck and the stream had not shrunken.

In a patch of aspens on the bank, well concealed in a crotch, he found a deserted robin's nest. Part of the inner wall of mud had crumbled on one side, but most of the lining of fine grass was still intact and made an inviting bed.

The Squirrel jumped in to try it. But he stayed only a few minutes. The restless leaves around him, constantly quivering and quaking, bothered him. He was a child of the evergreen forest, used to the dignified silence of needles even when branches swayed. How could he sleep in the midst of musky aspen leaves that trembled with the slightest stir of air?

Cautiously he leaped along the bank to a venerable limber pine, then to a clump of Engelmann spruces near a bend in the stream. Almost at once he caught the lingering scent of a squirrel on the tree trunks and along the branches. In the tallest tree he found an abandoned nest full of fairly fresh squirrel smell. Broken and battered by the hailstorm, the nest had not been repaired.

He darted to the treetop to look for cones, but not a single one hung from the branches. Evidently the owner of the nest had left because of the crop failure in the treetops.

The Squirrel was hungry. Since leaving the newly found grove early that afternoon, he had eaten nothing but a butterfly and a grasshopper. Cautiously he jerked down the spruce, pausing as usual to look around before making the final leap to the ground.

In the gray dusk settling over the valley he found a clump of lupine that had gone to seed. He filled his mouth with seeds and scrambled back to the abandoned nest to eat them. Then he curled up to sleep.

Most of the nervous tension of his adventure was over. He had found cones, plenty of cones! They grew on tall thin lodgepole pines in another valley, a mile or two below another beaver pond, where water still flowed in spite of the drought. For some reason he did not understand, cones of all ages, some five and ten years old, still clung tightly to the trees. Many of the cones had weathered open, but others still contained numerous small seeds. Although new cones were not plentiful, in the midst of the abundance from other years they were not missed.

Finding the grove was, of course, only the first step. Now he must lead his family there, and harvest his winter food supply before too many squirrels congregated in the grove. How different the lodgepole pines were from the trees of his forest, where cones freed their seeds each year!

Some time before midnight he was awakened by the sound of feet splashing and plodding down the stream bed. Alert at once, he pricked up his ears to listen. The travelers sounded clumsy of foot. He heard the whimpering of youngsters and encouraging sounds urging them on. Who would be passing so noisily in the night, and why?

Curious as always, he poked his head from the nest and peered down. A waning moon in the east lit the narrow valley flanked by dark masses of trees. Moonlight glinted on streaks of water between the rocks.

But branches hindered his view. He could see movement, a number of dark shapes humping along. Porcupines waddled something like that. Yet he had rarely seen more than one porcupine at a time, never more than two—a mother and a young one.

Just then the breeze brought him a scent, the same scent he had smelled on the roof of the beaver house that day the marten chased him. Beavers were traveling through the night, away from the pond.

"Hoo, hoo-hoo, hoo, hoo," came the eerie hunting cry of an owl. Frightened, the Squirrel ducked back into the nest, knowing from experience that an owl could make his voice sound far-away and impossible to locate. The Squirrel had taken a chance, looking out. The glint of moonlight on his eyes might easily give away his hiding place to a watchful owl.

For some time the Squirrel's sharp ears followed the progress of the beavers as they plodded down the stream bed. He heard the owl hoot again, heard a rabbit squeal in fright. Then all was still, until the yapping of coyotes echoed between the hills. Finally he dropped off to sleep once more.

Soon after dawn he was back at his homestead.

Food seemed more scarce than ever after his visit to the lodgepole grove. The hailstorm had finished the devastating work of the drought by battering growing things on the forest floor. The low blueberry bushes and flower stalks were shorn of most of their leaves. In the marsh, willow and alder shrubs were shredded, and bistort and sedge and marsh grass still lay flattened on the ground. Yet in spite of the scarcity of food, in spite of knowing where cones could be found in abundance, the Squirrel was reluctant to abandon his home.

This group of trees had always been the center of his world. He knew intimately every branch of every tree, every stone and log and juniper patch on the ground beneath, every seedling at various stages of growth. Here he had harvested four crops of cones and buried them in secret storehouses; here he had mated, and built nests, and watched his young grow up.

All day he lingered in the well-loved place, dreading to make the break. He saw his mate watching him expectantly, ready to follow as soon as he gave the signal.

The next day he spent considerable time on the ground, sniffing around, looking for a last feast while he postponed the time of departure. Finally, under the far end of his midden pile, buried beneath shucks of cobs, he unearthed a little cache of cones he had forgotten. He called jubilantly to his mate.

The unexpected feast called for a nap, and then the sun blazed too hot and bright for pleasant traveling. And then . . . who would think of setting out on a long journey with dusk coming on?

They finally started at noon the next day. And once started, the Squirrel pressed ahead without a backward look at his homestead.

He led the way south, skirting the marsh and entering the valley below the beaver pond. It would be folly for five squirrels, three of them young and inexperienced, to try to cross an open place where enemies could strike from all sides. They must stick to the treetops at all costs, even though it meant long detours.

Below the beaver pond he followed the bank of the little stream that sparkled among the rocks, flowing downgrade away from the heights.

After making the final break with his home trees, the Squirrel's one purpose was to reach the lodgepoles as quickly as possible. He scolded the youngsters impatiently. Midway in their fourth month, they scampered along agilely enough at first. But they soon tired. And they often hesitated over leaps from one tree to the next. He waved his tail angrily and flounced ahead.

When he reached the clump of spruces where he had spent the night, he stopped to show his mate the deserted nest. She sniffed around it, piecing the story together. Then with surprise he saw her herd the youngsters into the nest for a rest. A rest so soon! Chattering his protest, he sat on a limb and gave his mate a piece of his mind. She groomed her paws, unheeding.

As they waited in the tree, another pine squirrel, traveling alone, caught up with them and passed. He was the first of a number of squirrels they saw traveling away from the heights that day.

Soon the squirrel family was on its way again, following the winding treetop road along the stream bank.

The Squirrel saw the hawk while waiting in a spruce for his family to catch up with him. First he saw the dark shadow gliding across sun-brightened rocks of the stream bed. Then, looking up, he caught sight of a large squirrel-catching, bird-catching hawk sailing over the valley.

At once the Squirrel screamed the alarm in an urgent voice as he whirled around the tree trunk. The bird's short wings were adapted to flight through branches that were not too bushy, and the squirrels must get under cover to be safe. It had been a mistake to follow the stream bed so closely. He should have taken the longer way through deep woods. Calling another warning to his mate and the young ones, he darted from the bank to the shadows of the woods.

Confident that he could dodge the hawk if it swooped, the Squirrel kept up his alarm call, to give his family time to find refuge in bushy branches.

But the hawk did not choose to strike at the noisy Squirrel. With amazing speed and skill it swooped through the tree on the bank where the three young ones scuttled close to their mother. The sound of rushing wind in feathers gave frightening warning. Strike!

Somehow the youngsters managed to elude the grasping talons. The hawk rose to roll in the air and swoop again.

"Chickaree-chickaree," cried the Squirrel, over and over, in a fury of anger. He could see the flash of light on the

hawk's breast as it swung on a tilt toward the treetops, ready to strike again.

Another lightning swoop! The hawk hurtled through the branches with unbelievable dexterity. This time it rose with one of the panic-stricken youngsters in its claws. The body hung limp as the hawk flew off over the treetops.

The Squirrel knew he must whisk the rest of his family to a safer place before the hawk returned. Even though it meant a longer journey, he must lead the way to the lodgepoles through deeper woods and denser shadows. Quickly he piloted his mate and young ones away from the stream.

Now there were only four making their way to the lodgepole grove. The Squirrel accepted the loss of his youngster as he accepted drought and other calamities. Young ones came and young ones went. In a month or two the surviving youngsters would strike out on their own. The Squirrel and his mate would probably never see them again. That was the way of life.

The swing away from the stream delayed them and by midafternoon the Squirrel knew they could not reach the lodgepoles before dark. Already the young ones were whimpering with weariness, and dusk fell quickly at this time of year. The best they could do would be to cross the rocky ridge to the north of the stream and drop into the next valley to spend the night.

The sun had set and a sparkle of September coolness was creeping over the mountains by the time the squirrels reached a gentle slope on the other side of the ridge. The slope, covered with aspens and a sprinkling of evergreens, dipped to a beaver pond.

Stopping in one of the spruces, the Squirrel looked around for a likely sleeping place. He spotted a large bird's nest high in a limber pine with spreading branches. But he saw something else that made him hesitate—a dark-colored hump on one of the lower branches. Two nests in the same tree? Or was the lower one a parasitic growth bunching the needles into a ball? Warily he scampered over to investigate.

The strong scent that filled his nostrils even before he leaped into the pine explained the mystery. A porcupine was asleep on the lower limb, waiting for night to come, when he would lumber down for a drink and a few nibbles of something besides pine bark. The smell of the porky's greasy unkempt coat made the Squirrel's sensitive nostrils twitch.

He stared at the dark hump of fur and quills. He was not afraid. A porcupine was to be avoided, not feared. So far as the Squirrel knew, the slow-moving creature had never caused the squirrel clan any trouble.

He leaped to a branch above the porcupine and hurried to look at the nest. In a way, sleeping in a porcupine tree had its advantages. Squirrel scent would be covered by the stronger porcupine smell. And, except as a last resort, none of the Squirrel's enemies would climb a tree to attack a porcupine.

Bits of bark flew from under the Squirrel's claws as he scampered up the trunk, but the porky did not stir. He had as little concern about squirrels as about birds flitting in and out of the branches all day.

The nest, built by nutcrackers, was in good condition and amply large for the Squirrel and his family. On its bulky base of small sticks the true nest of the interwoven moss and dried grasses and strips of bark lay waiting to be used. He called out the good news.

Dusk filled the grove by the time his mate and the weary young ones were bedded down. The last flickers of daylight began to fade on the open pond. Feeling unusually safe in a strange place, with the porcupine on a limb below and the tree full of its smell, the Squirrel sat in the twilight, listening and looking. Already home seemed far away. A strange new life lay ahead. A feeling of excitement and suspense now overbalanced his tie to the past, to the familiar and known.

In the grayness of the darkening pond he caught the movement of two beavers swimming toward shore, followed by widening V-shaped ripples glinting with silver. A stir of breeze sent aspen leaves from nearby trees rattling to the ground. They had dried early after the summer of little rain.

One strong wind, and the ground would be covered with them.

Some time in the night the Squirrel was awakened by a strange noise near his tree. The sky was alive with stars, the night calm and cool. A chipping, chipping sound came from below, near the aspens. Bits of something kept striking the ground. "Chip, chip. Chip, chip." For a long time the noise went on without a pause. The Squirrel's mate stirred; she was listening, too.

The Squirrel drew himself to the edge of the nest to peer over. What was making that noise? Had the porky found an old antler to gnaw on?

In the moonlight the open ground between the trees looked lightly snowed upon, almost frosted over. But he knew it was moon-frost.

With a quick movement, the Squirrel dislodged a stick from the outside wall of the nest. It clattered down through the branches, and the clicking, chipping noise stopped. Soon it started again.

Suddenly something cracked. The Squirrel could hear clumsy feet hurry over newly fallen leaves. Crash! With a shake of fluttery leaves, an aspen fell to the ground. The scent of beaver wafted up to the nest.

So it was only a beaver cutting an aspen in the middle of the night! The Squirrel settled back to sleep. There was no accounting for the strange ways of some wild folk!

Let Winter Come

1

WITH HER FIRST DIVE into the pond, the Beaver felt that they had found a safe new home. How different the world looked just one night away from the old pond! Here lay fresh cool water handy to an aspen slope where hailstones had not shorn the trees of leaves.

Half the pond twinkled with the light of the waning moon and early-morning stars, half of it lay in the shadow of the nearby hill.

Slowly, inquisitively, the Beaver swam toward the shadow, keeping close to her exhausted kits. She knew that they would soon revive in the water.

Now they were safe, they were all safe, except for the limping yearling who had disappeared on the ridge. In her excitement the memory of him was already fading. The old life was over, a new life was beginning. . . .

Suddenly she stopped swimming. Ahead, on the shadowy side of the pond, loomed a beaver house. Was the pond already occupied, then? Was this just a resting place before their journey must continue?

Although the Beaver had begun the dangerous journey with no picture in her mind of what the new homesite would be like, she had not expected her mate to lead them to a pond

135

where another family already lived. Treading water, she waited to see what he would do. Perhaps he had already visited this pond and made friends with the beavers . . .

Dark heads, followed by moonlit ripples, were coming toward them. The Beaver purred softly to her kits and yearlings, and they waited beside her. Her mate swam confidently ahead.

As she waited, she sniffed the refreshing air moving down the valley. She heard the gentle trickle of water over the dam at the lower end of the pond and the reassuring sound of a stream flowing in at the upper end. Glints of moonlight showed a short canal leading through a stretch of low ground to the foot of the aspen slope. A sizable beaver house rose from the shadows. Everything about the site pointed to the industry of the family living there and the well-being of the valley, in spite of a summer of little rain.

She saw her mate swimming back with the beavers. Soon she was touching noses with a young mother followed by a string of curious yearlings and kits. A grizzled old grandfather swam up, aloof but not unfriendly.

The Beaver looked for the head of the family, knowing that without his approval they would not be able to stay in the pool. Surely, even if he had been working in the aspens, he must have heard the joyful splashes of the newcomers when they reached the pond. Yet he did not appear.

The yearlings of both families began to play together, chasing and diving through the water. The kits, more timid, hovered in their mothers' shadows.

By the next night no father beaver had put in an appearance. The Beaver had been on the lookout for him, swimming around the pond and up the short canal, watching and listening.

Finally it dawned on her that the family must be father-less. Perhaps the young male beaver had failed to return from his summer jaunt, or had been killed after his return by a lurking enemy or a falling tree. All she knew was that the young mother was carrying on alone, looking after the grandfather and a number of kits and yearlings.

By the second night it was clear that the Beaver's mate intended to stay at the pond. He began looking for a place to build a lodge, churring for her to join him. Together they swam slowly and carefully around the pond and underwater, crisscrossing the bottom.

Her mate had made a wise choice in leading them to this pond. With summer nearing its end, how would there have been time to dam a stream, build a house, and gather a win-ter's food supply before cold weather set in? Here the pond lay full and safe, and the other beavers were friendly.

Signs of drought showed all around—in the short grasses and flower stalks on the bank, in prematurely dry aspen leaves already shaking to the ground with every breeze, in the stunted shrubs beyond the stream. Yet two strong springs still welled up on the pond bottom, and a fair-sized stream of mountain water still flowed in from the head of the valley.

The beavers' eyes were too nearsighted to see the dark unbroken mass of pines, spruces, and firs sprawling up the slopes beyond the pond. And even if they had seen them, the beavers could not have made the connection between a thriving forest and the well-being of wild folk.

No forest fire had ruined the high slopes of this valley. Great trees cooled the summer wind blowing across sun-struck rock masses on the mountainside; the absorbent car-pet of the forest floor caught and held the moisture of melting snowdrifts and rain. The moisture sank slowly down,

down to supply roots and to seep into seams in the granite, eventually feeding the two springs in the beaver pond. Little water evaporated under the shady roof of the forest.

The stream brought some seepage from the forest, but mostly it carried melted ice and snow from a smaller glacier between rugged peaks. No matter how hot the summer, this patch of ice and snow, almost a hundred feet deep, kept feeding the stream with a cold, dependable supply of water.

Looking at the new homesite, the Beaver could see only one drawback. Aspens were not as handy nor as abundant as at the other pond.

All the near aspens on the slope had already been cut by several generations of beavers. Beyond the dead gray stubs, aspens and limber pines and spruces grew together, fluttery leaves against dark needles, slender gray tree-stems among dark trunks. The Beaver and her mate would have to drag aspens for the winter storage pile quite a distance. That involved danger.

But the Beaver's first concern was a home.

In their exploration of the pond, she and her mate discovered the ideal location for a lodge—near the second spring, across the pond from the house of the other family. Her mate started work on the foundation immediately, fetching sticks and scooping up mud from the pond bottom.

But finishing a lodge before the pond would freeze was out of the question. Building just the massive foundation-platform to reach above water level would take nights and nights of work. Then more nights would be needed for building the dome-shaped room on top of the platform and connecting it, by a tunnel, to the pond. Meanwhile the family needed a safe place to sleep and take refuge.

Leaving her mate to his self-imposed task of working on

the foundation, the Beaver swam around the pond again. She must find a place to dig a simple den in the bank. Then, after aspens for the storage pile had been cut and firmly anchored in the pond, they could all work on the lodge until the pond froze over.

She needed a high bank, so the den would be above water level, in a spot where digging would not be too difficult. Such a place was hard to find. The only high bank, across the pond from the aspen grove, looked rocky and unpromising for digging. Besides, it lay some distance from the spring where they would anchor their food pile. Still, she had no choice.

Even before dusk, she set to work digging a tunnel to slant up from the bottom of the pond to the high bank. She had little difficulty in prying stones from the moist soil. One by one she carried them to the dam, out of the way.

Soon her mate swam over to see what she was doing. She kept on digging her tunnel. Before she knew it he was helping, as if he shared her eagerness to have a roof over the family's head. He even swam to fetch sticks he had gathered for the lodge foundation, to line the tunnel walls and keep them from caving in.

They made good progress as long as the earth was wet. But when they reached dry ground, above water level, they ran into trouble. Here the soil, almost as hard as stone after the dry summer, cemented the boulders in place. Claw as they would, the beavers could not loosen some of the boulders. Worse than that, the biggest of them lay too close together for even a small room to be scooped out between them. Just as they were making progress, the unyielding face of another big rock would appear.

The Beaver surfaced and headed for a low spot on the

shore where she could scramble up. Somehow, they must find a place without boulders where they could dig a den big enough for two grown beavers and four youngsters.

She could hear the yearlings of the two families playing together in the pond. The kits she had left under willow branches overhanging the bank, where they would be safe and out of sight while she worked.

Sniffing and listening, to be sure that all was well, the Beaver drifted near the shore. The rank smell of greasy fur came to her, and the sound of clumsy footsteps. A porcupine was waddling along the bank. She had no fear of porcupines, but no fondness for them either, so she waited patiently until the clumsy one moved on through the night.

Shuffling, with her nose close to the ground, she soon discovered a place almost free of boulders, somewhat back from the rocky bank. Unfortunately the ground there sloped in the wrong direction. Digging the den-room would be easier, but to get enough head room the beavers would have to work too close to the surface. What would prevent a cave-in if some heavy animal like a deer bounded over the ground?

She hesitated, then sniffed over the ground again. Suddenly she scampered to the pond.

In a short time she was back, waddling on her hind feet, carrying all the mud she could hold against her breast with her forepaws. Again and again she went for mud, piling it on the rock-free place. Now, as when she was a kit, she liked the soft smooth feel of mud oozing through her forepaws. She liked dipping her paws into it and patting it in place.

Before she swam up the stream to find sticks, she brought her mate to see what she was doing.

Soon he, too, was carrying sticks and mud; and before long the yearlings were helping. Slowly the low-domed top of a beaver house began to take shape on the rock-free place back from the pond.

This dome would give the beavers headroom in a den underneath. Now instead of trying to make a room between boulders, they could use the space for a passageway and dig their den under the sticks and mud, in the rock-free ground. It meant digging a longer tunnel, but the den would be larger and more comfortable and better ventilated. There they would be safe until they could finish their lodge in the spring.

While her mate and yearlings worked on the roof, the Beaver went back to lengthen the tunnel and scoop out the den.

In a few days they had a snug burrow. Instead of a water-door in the middle of the floor, as in the old lodge, they had a dry tunnel entrance at one side. Not until the tunnel sloped down to the level of the pond was it filled with water.

The den finished, and beds of shredded bark and grass in place, the Beaver and her mate faced their next big task. They knew from cutting aspens for their current needs that the sap was beginning to run, beginning to start down to the roots before winter set in. Instinct and experience told them that harvesting must be done at just the right time—when enough sap had left the bark so that it would not spoil in the underwater storage pile, yet before so much sap had gone that the thick bark would be dry and hard to peel.

Now, with the sap at the right stage, the time had come for the beavers to start harvesting.

The trees had begun to change color soon after the beavers reached the new pond. By daylight the slope fluttered with a strange brightness when the wind blew; by starlight silvery round leaves tinkled and drifted to the ground.

Although the other beavers had already started their harvest, they made slow progress without a strong adult male to help. The old grandfather was hampered in cutting because of a broken chisel tooth. This meant that most of the work of cutting fell to the lot of the young mother. Every night she worked industriously, while the grandfather took charge of anchoring the logs and branches in the pond. Both he and the yearlings dragged branches and lengths of tree trunks down the slope to the canal, and even the kits helped float branches from the canal to the site of the storage pile.

The Beaver and her mate chose to do their cutting on the slope near the dam, so as not to interfere with the other family. It meant dragging branches and trunk-lengths a longer distance, without a canal handy; and it meant working too far from water for safety. But danger went hand in hand with harvesting.

The Beaver enjoyed sinking her teeth into an aspen trunk and chiseling out the chips. The taste of the bark and texture of the soft wood pleased her; besides, chisel teeth never ceased growing, and biting kept them worn down to the proper length.

To lessen the risk in working so far from the pond, the Beaver posted one of the yearlings on shore and the other on the dam to give a warning whack with their tails at the first hint of danger.

It took her almost an hour of chipping and gnawing to cut an aspen four or five inches in diameter. Then she had to trim off the larger branches, gnaw the trunk into manageable lengths, and maneuver them to the pond. Even with the best of luck, and with both of them working most of the night, it would take the Beaver and her mate several weeks to cut enough aspens for the long winter months.

She worked doggedly, eager to get the job done, yet ever conscious of the dangers. When the night was bright enough to see the top of the tree, she studied it before beginning to cut, to be sure no branches were entangled in another tree-top. When it was too dark to see, she had to take her chances. Sitting on her haunches, propped by her tail, she would put her forelegs against the tree and begin the long job by taking several quick bites. Reaching higher, she would take several more bites. Carefully she split out the space between.

Below and above, below and above she bit, sometimes tilting her head obliquely to break away the chips. She cut

mostly from one side of the tree. When it cracked a warning that it was about to fall, she ran for safety.

Early in the harvesting, her mate embedded a partly trimmed sapling in the mud near the second spring. To this he hooked and interlaced small aspen trees and branches as a start of the storage pile. Later he would weight the branches down with sections of trunk.

On the fifth night of harvesting, something happened that brought a great change to the pond.

Before going ashore for the night's work, the Beaver always swam quietly around for a while to make sure that all was well. She had been surprised that the pond was so free of enemies. No shadow of eagle or hawk had appeared by day, and so far no owl had hooted at night. Several times coyotes had loitered on the bank, and the sound of their yapping often echoed down the valley, but they had not interfered with the beavers' work. Once or twice she had sniffed a strong cat smell, and stayed in the pond for safety.

This night she and her mate were harvesting aspens well up the slope. Suddenly, as they chipped away at the soft wood, they heard an agonizing trouble-cry coming from farther along the slope, near the canal. The yearling they had left near the dam as sentinel dove into the pond with a whack; almost immediately came the warning sound of the other yearling who had been dragging branches.

The Beaver and her mate raced for the pond as fast as their clumsy legs could carry them.

Hurrying to the den, they found the yearlings and kits safe in the tunnel. They shooed them up into the den, and swam on to the beaver lodge to see if the other family was safe.

Frightened youngsters were huddled together on the sleeping shelf. Where was their mother? Where was the grandfather?

The Beaver and her mate sculled back down the tunnel to the pond to investigate. Quietly they skimmed along the dark surface, eyes, ears and noses alert. Near the canal entrance they found the old grandfather watching and waiting, still as a floating log.

For a long time the three beavers listened and waited, then swam around the pond reconnoitering. After the frightening cry they had heard, they were afraid to go ashore. They strained their ears to catch the footfall of an enemy; they twitched their noses to catch a scent. Staring into the darkness, they tried to penetrate the shadows on the bank to see what lay beyond . . .

They waited and watched, but the young mother did not come home.

No one worked any more that night.

Not until early the next morning, before the light of the rising sun sparkled on the pond, did the Beaver piece together what had happened. She saw the old grandfather gather enough courage to scramble ashore near the canal leading to the foot of the aspen slope, heard him shuffling around, watched him return safely to the pond. This gave her courage to swim to the bank, herself.

A patch of dark fur clinging to a log, a trail of dried blood, an abandoned sapling, and the lingering scent of a mountain lion told the story. The young mother had been dragging a sapling to the canal when the waiting lion had pounced on her.

The Beaver swam immediately to the orphaned young ones in the lodge. She nuzzled them, churred to them, tried to comfort them in every way she knew. Her own family was so small now. She would gladly take these youngsters and raise them as her own.

The kits leaned against her; the yearlings did not back away. For some time she stayed, mothering them. Then she went for her own young ones and brought them to the beaver lodge.

With the help of the grandfather and the yearlings, the Beaver and her mate finished the storage pile near the lodge before cold weather struck. Several nights they could not work because the mountain lion came back. Another night coyotes yapped around the pond. But before a cold October wind tore the last leaves from the aspens, the job was done.

They all lived together in the beaver lodge now, everyone happily adjusted to the change except the old grandfather. So many yearlings and kits underfoot irritated him. For a while he grumbled and mumbled about it; then he disappeared.

The Beaver swam around looking for him. Finally she found him in bachelor quarters, in the den in the bank. There he would spend the winter, keeping himself company, with occasional visits to the lodge and games with the young ones under the ice.

Satisfied, she swam back to the house. A cold wind was rumpling the top of the pond, churning it into little waves with whitecaps. She thrust up her nose to sniff the air. Sharp crystals of snow driven before the wind stung her head. The summer of little rain, the summer of uncertainty and challenge had come to an end.

2

Within sight of the lodgepole grove, the Squirrel stopped in a treetop at the edge of a natural mountain meadow. He already knew about the meadow. On his former trip, both going and coming, he had made a wide detour to avoid it. Now as he reached the edge of the woods with his hungry family, he hesitated. Petulantly he waved his tail.

Ahead he could see the wide-spreading stand of lodgepole pines. He could hear the noisy barking of squirrels, disputing the possession of trees. From the sound it was obvious that dozens of squirrels had already come from miles around to establish themselves in the grove.

Impatiently the Squirrel listened to their chatter. Might it not be worth while to take a chance and dash across the meadow, to be sure of getting a place? More squirrels were on their way from the upper forests.

The detour would be safer, of course. But the sight of the food-trees so close, and the noise of rivals already enjoying the cones, excited him. He and his family were hungry, and his instinct for speedy harvesting of the winter supply of food cried out to be satisfied.

As he hesitated he saw two squirrels, a young one following a hoary old one, enter a nearby tree. The old one stopped for a moment to get his bearings, then at once turned north to make the detour. The young one looked after him without making a move to follow. Instead, he twitched his ears toward the squirrel sounds coming from the grove, leaped to a tree at the edge of the meadow, and ran down the trunk. After a hasty look around, as he clung head-down to the trunk, he jumped to the dry grass. With eager bounds he flashed toward the grove.

Out of the shadows at the edge of the woods leaped a large animal with a bushy tail. A coyote! He had been lying in wait for foolish squirrels to show themselves in the open. His legs stretched in great bounds as he dashed across the grass.

The Squirrel watched from the tree, his eyes bulging, his tail high but quiet, one forepaw drawn up against his chest.

Hearing the sound of feet bounding behind him, the young squirrel panicked. For a split second he stopped, gripped by terror, trying to decide whether to race ahead or turn back to the safety of the trees. He lost his chance to do either. With a pounce the coyote was upon him.

And at that moment the Squirrel saw, without moving his head, a hawk swinging over the meadow. Enemies on the ground and enemies in the sky!

Keeping so still they seemed part of the trees, the Squirrel and his family waited tensely. They saw the coyote carry his victim to the woods and disappear behind a brush pile. They saw the hawk's banking wings catch a flash of sunlight as they swept close to the opening, saw his gleaming eyes search the grass for another sign of life. Then the hawk swung up again and disappeared.

The Squirrel could see that a price would have to be paid for the food that lay ahead. As hungry squirrels came to claim the cones, enemies would follow. Hawks would swoop down from the sky for several weeks yet, before flying to lower altitudes for the winter. Martens and weasels, coyotes and bobcats, and owls would stay all winter, lurking in and around the busy grove. The Squirrel would have to be even more vigilant than he had been in the spruce forest.

He led his family to the grove by a long detour, through the densest branches he could find.

He expected trouble as soon as they reached the lodge-poles, not so much from enemies as from squirrels already in possession. To claim a domain of even a few trees, the Squirrel was prepared to fight. He jumped into the first of the cone-laden trees with his tail fluffed out, his fur bristling, in an effort to make himself look formidable.

Nothing happened. No one noticed him. Barking encouragingly to his mate, he squatted on a limb and reached for a late breakfast.

The lodgepole cones were small, about the size of Engelmann spruce cones but rounder and rougher. Even the low dead branches of the trees had cones clinging to them, but most of these were half weathered-away and empty of seeds. Higher in the treetops, on living branches, cones of different ages clung, many of them still intact with their fruit hidden away.

The Squirrel pulled a cone from a living branch and began to shuck off the scales. Getting at the tiny seeds, between scales sealed over with a coat of resin, was not easy, but seeds were seeds and they were worth working for.

Instead of hanging down as on spruces and Douglas firs, or standing upright as on balsam firs, the cones of the lodge-poles grew at irregular angles, tightly attached to the bark of a branch. The Squirrel often found them hard to loosen.

The youngsters teased to be fed, and their mother gave them a lesson in loosening the resin-coated scales from the cones. Soon they would have to forage for themselves. Soon they would be on their own.

As the Squirrel ate, he sniffed at the unfamiliar smells in the lodgepole grove—the warm smell of sunlight on pine needles and on prematurely dry aspen leaves, the dusty smell of bark and old cones. He missed the penetrating fragrance of his forest, the strong incense of fir and spruce needles. All his life that invigorating spiciness had been part of the air he breathed.

Yet the lodgepoles held life-saving cones! Greedily the Squirrel plucked out the seeds and nibbled them. Why these trees should bear when his beloved forest lay barren was a question he could not answer. It was beyond his range of knowledge that a forest fire, almost sixty years before, had made way for this grove of closely packed trees in the first place.

Fire at the head of his home valley, above the range of lodgepoles, had brought nothing but disaster: it had ruined the homesteads and food supply of many wild folk; it had destroyed soil accumulated through the centuries; it had exposed slopes to erosion by water and wind.

Seeds of the high-altitude trees had not been able to withstand the heat of the fire and had perished. A few seeds buried away in squirrel storehouses survived, but when they sprouted the seedlings had no chance of growing. Unable to stand the excessive light and exposure of the fire-swept slopes, they gave up before they really started. It would take many years for high-altitude trees to creep slowly back up the fire-ravaged slopes.

But in the lower valley where the Squirrel had migrated, the forest fire had brought only temporary disaster when it raged through a mixed stand of pines, aspens, and Douglas firs many years before. Thousands of trees fell and burned in the sweep of the fire, and the seeds of all but the lodgepoles perished. Some aspen roots remained unharmed and sent up shoots.

Sealed under the tight scales of the cones and covered by a thick coating of resin wax, lodgepole seeds actually benefited from the fire. As the resin melted, the scales opened from the heat. Seeds that had been imprisoned for years were freed and popped out in great numbers. Wind scattered them. They took root in ground where other seeds could not grow. Thousands upon thousands of lodgepole seedlings sprang up on every acre of the burnt-over land. They thrived on heat and light, even on lack of humus. As time went on many were crowded out, yet thousands remained, growing close together, stretching pole-like trunks to the sun.

Now the grove was an island of plenty in a sea of drought. Cones hung on the trees for the taking, and the Squirrel was willing to fight for them.

Strangely enough, few squirrels in the grove were fighting. They chattered and fussed, they waved their tails and stomped their forefeet, they darted in and out of branches and chased and barked. Yet few actually made an attack. Even the Squirrel did nothing more than scold when a newcomer leaped into the tree where the family was eating. As a newcomer himself, he lacked the feeling of ownership that entitled him to fight. First he must hunt out a little group of trees and claim them for his own.

A breeze had sprung up, enough to make the leaves of a nearby aspen flutter and dance, yet not enough to move the long thin shadows on the ground beneath the lodgepoles. How different the slender shadow-streaks looked from the mottled patches under his old trees! For a moment a wave of homesickness swept over him, but only for a moment.

After eating his fill, the Squirrel scampered around to

find the trees where he wanted to settle. He whisked from one tree to another, ignoring the scoldings of irate neighbors. Finally he found a little group of unclaimed lodgepoles that pleased him. He whickered to his mate.

He felt impelled to start harvesting cones at once. Eagerly he worked to loosen the cones from the branches, throwing them to the ground with an outward jerk of his head. His mate came to help. As the cones bounced down through the branches, she scurried to gather them in piles.

So strong was the squirrels' instinct for harvesting and storing, it did not occur to them that cones which had already weathered many a winter on the tree could be depended upon to weather another, that cones would be there for plucking whenever mealtime arrived. The desire to harvest was so tightly woven into the squirrels' life-pattern they could not let an autumn pass without hoarding a food supply.

Boisterous nutcrackers cawed around the grove, stealing cones cut by the squirrels, even swooping down and seizing them out of their paws. On the ground chipmunks whisked away cones that had been cut and dropped. The grove hummed with activity.

And then the marten came!

The Squirrel, busily occupied with his harvesting, suddenly saw another squirrel racing madly toward his tree. Behind him came the leaping, flashing dark shape that struck terror into the heart of every small creature of the woods. A pine marten! On its chest and throat a light-colored patch showed like a flag of warning.

The Squirrel's one impulse was to get out of the way as fast as his agile legs could carry him. With a whisk and a bound he landed in the next tree, then dashed on to the next . . . just as the other squirrel took a desperate leap for an aspen branch too slender to sustain the weight of his pursuer. Without hesitating, the marten swerved, changed its course, and leaped through the lodgepoles after the Squirrel.

The race was on.

The Squirrel streaked toward the middle of the grove, into the midst of the confusion. In strange trees his one hope was to shake the marten from his trail, even as the other squirrel had done. Flash, dash, up and down they raced, their sharp claws, like barbs of steel, gripping trunk and branch and sending bits of bark flying. Turning and twisting around tree trunks, leaping and climbing, they tore through the stubby branches of the close-growing trees.

Although a number of squirrels scattered before them, the marten did not swerve from its course again. No matter how the Squirrel twisted and swirled, the marten stuck to his trail. And slowly but surely the marten was gaining.

The Squirrel dashed blindly ahead at full speed, not knowing where to look for safety in the strange woods. Where was a leap too broad for the marten? A branch too light to hold it? A door-hole too small for it to enter?

The Squirrel was tiring; he could not keep up the pace much longer. Ahead he glimpsed the weathered trunk of an old dead pine. His experience with dead trees gave him courage to take a desperate chance. Surely there would be a woodpecker hole, a flicker hole . . .

With a burst of energy generated by desperate need, the Squirrel dashed through a dozen treetops, down a trunk, across a small opening, and up the dead tree. He could hear the marten closing in behind him, shortening the distance with every powerful bound.

Whisk! Just in time the Squirrel dove into a woodpecker hole.

He tumbled into an empty nest some distance below the hole. His heart pounded furiously from the exertion of his flight. Above the pounding and his gasps for breath he could hear the marten snarling and hissing as it scratched at the hole, trying to tear its way in.

The Squirrel had eluded martens before, but never under such gruelling circumstances. His escapes had been in the dense-topped firs, and spruces with sweeping branches leading from one tree to the next. The branches of the lodgepoles were stubby because the trees grew so close together and, lacking dip and resiliency, they felt strange beneath his feet.

Not until the marten grew tired of tearing at the wood around the hole did the Squirrel relax and sink into the nest of dried grass that smelled of old mouse and fresh squirrel. He heard his enemy give a final snarl and run down the trunk.

For some time the Squirrel lay quietly, gathering his strength. Now he knew what he must do when he found his way back to his mate. Before cutting any more cones, before burying the cones he had already cut, he must find a place of safety near his trees.

With so many squirrels in the grove, woodpecker holes would be at a premium. He could not hope to possess one without having to fight for it continually. He must find some other place nearer his trees with a doorway too small for a marten to enter, too strong for a coyote to tear apart, too hidden for a hawk or owl to find.

He zigzagged back to his mate.

Immediately he began exploring the trees he had chosen

and the ground beneath, bit by bit. A nest in the treetops would not be practical for winter when cold winds swept down from the mountains. The long slender trunks would sway and knock their tops against each other.

The ground beneath his trees seemed unusually bare of places to hide. There were few logs. In a grove where trunks grew so close together, dead trees had no place to fall. Often they caught in crotches or branches and stood slanting there, without falling.

Patches of sprawling evergreen kinnikinnick, with berries beginning to ripen, grew under the trees and offered concealment from the searching eyes of hawks. But four-footed enemies could trace a squirrel's scent into the trailing shrubs and ferret him out.

Finally the Squirrel settled on digging a burrow between two close-growing lodgepole roots. He had never dug a burrow before, only tunnels in snowdrifts, yet he knew how to do it. By clawing the dirt loose with his forepaws and pushing it back with his hind feet, he soon had a good start on a tunnel between the protecting roots.

Dusk fell on the grove before his tunnel was deep enough for him to make a turn and hollow out a burrow-den. The noisy chatter of squirrels ceased. By the time he scrambled up to a tree crotch, his mate and youngsters had already found a place of their own to hide for the night.

He slept uneasily without a roof to cover him. Night noises were as different in the grove as the smells. He could hear the stream running nearby, closer than the stream that fed the old beaver pond. The continual movement of aspen leaves at the edge of the grove drowned out little sounds he was used to listening for even in his sleep—the click of

weasel claws on bark, the louder claw-scratch of a marten
or bobcat.

An owl hooted. Then another. That sound was familiar
enough. The owls, like the squirrels' other enemies, were
gathering near the grove. He hunched down.

The next day the Squirrel dug a room at the end of his
extended tunnel—not a large room, but big enough for four
if the young ones chose to stay. He chirred to his mate to
come look. She ran in and out with a buzz of approval, and
began to gather dry grass and leaves for a bed.

Shelter provided, the Squirrel's harvesting instinct engulfed him once more. He scurried to one of the piles of
cones his mate had collected. In the matted trash near his

burrow entrance, he scratched out a shallow storage place for several dozen cones. With dry trash above and below they would be well ventilated. Tamping the covering back into place with his feet and snout, he moved to the base of a big lichen-covered boulder to dig his second storehouse.

A dry breeze blew from the mountains, whisking a few aspen leaves into the lodgepole grove. Fingers of sunlight found their way through the treetops and laid streaks of shadow on the ground. The Squirrel dashed up a tree trunk to perch on a limb and clean some sticky pitch from his leg. While he was at it, he carefully worked over the plume of his tail, cleaning and fluffing it. He was beginning to feel at home.

He saw his mate leading the youngsters through the lodgepoles, to get them used to the feel of the tall slim trees. As he turned back to his grooming, his eye fell on a branch next to him, laden with cones, the scales still tightly closed over the seeds. Here was food. Here was shelter. Let the wind blow and the snow fall! Here was a good place to spend the winter after the summer of little rain.

Selected Bibliography

Anthony, H. E.: *Field Book of North American Mammals*. New York: G. P. Putnam's Sons, 1928.

Ashton, Ruth E.: *Plants of Rocky Mountain National Park*. Washington, D.C.: United States Government Printing Office, 1933.

Buchsbaum, Ralph and Mildred: *Basic Ecology*. Pittsburgh: The Boxwood Press, 1957.

McCormick, Jack: *The Living Forest*. (Published in cooperation with The American Museum of Natural History.) New York: Harper & Brothers, 1959.

Mills, Enos A.: *In Beaver World*. Boston: Houghton Mifflin, 1913.

Mills, Enos A.: *Wild Animal Homesteads*. Boston: Houghton Mifflin, 1932.

Pearson, T. Gilbert (Editor-in-Chief): *Birds of America*. New York: Garden City Publishing Company, 1936.

Peattie, Donald Culross: *A Natural History of Western Trees*. Boston: Houghton Mifflin, 1953.

Seton, Ernest Thompson: *Lives of Game Animals*. New York: Doubleday, Doran & Company, 1929.

Storer, John H.: *The Web of Life, a First Book of Ecology*. New York: Devin-Adair, 1953.

Warren, Edward Royal: *The Mammals of Colorado, Their Habits and Distribution*. Norman, Okla.: University of Oklahoma Press, 1942.

c8